Inked Temptation

A MONTGOMERY INK: FORT COLLINS NOVEL

CARRIE ANN RYAN

Inked Temptation

A Montgomery Ink: Fort Collins Novel

By
Carrie Ann Ryan

Inked Temptation
A Montgomery Ink: Fort Collins Novel
By: Carrie Ann Ryan
© 2022 Carrie Ann Ryan
eBook ISBN 978-1-950443-78-9
Paperback ISBN 978-1-950443-79-6

Cover Art by Sweet N Spicy Designs
Photograph by Wander Aguilar

For my readers.
Thank you for becoming part of the Montgomerys.
Just know...this isn't the end.

Inked Temptation

This Montgomery finds his match in this touching second chance romance from NYT Bestselling Author Carrie Ann Ryan.

I thought I was moving on from my divorce, but now my ex is marrying someone else. I shouldn't be this broken up, but it's hard to put on a brave face when my family is basically an inked up Hallmark movie.

And I shouldn't be brooding about what I don't have, if it's going to cause me to fall off a roof. Right into the grumpy neighbor's burly arms.

He'd make a nice distraction, except he wants nothing to do with the burning attraction between us. Until one accidental kiss leads to more.

I'm not ready to risk my heart again, but Killian's tortured eyes don't seem to give me a choice. This thing between us is real.

But Killian is still trying to recover from a tragedy. And there are people who will do anything to make sure he never finds happiness again.

Praise for Carrie Ann Ryan

"Count on Carrie Ann Ryan for emotional, sexy, character driven stories that capture your heart!" – Carly Phillips, NY Times bestselling author

"Carrie Ann Ryan's romances are my newest addiction! The emotion in her books captures me from the very beginning. The hope and healing hold me close until the end. These love stories will simply sweep you away." ~ NYT Bestselling Author Deveny Perry

"Carrie Ann Ryan writes the perfect balance of sweet and heat ensuring every story feeds the soul." - Audrey Carlan, #1 New York Times Bestselling Author

"Carrie Ann Ryan never fails to draw readers in with passion, raw sensuality, and characters that pop off the page. Any book by Carrie Ann is an absolute treat." – New York Times Bestselling Author J. Kenner

"Carrie Ann Ryan knows how to pull your heartstrings and make your pulse pound! Her wonderful Redwood Pack series will draw you in and keep you reading long into the night. I can't wait to see what comes next with the new generation, the Talons. Keep them coming, Carrie Ann!" – Lara Adrian, New York Times bestselling author of CRAVE THE NIGHT

"With snarky humor, sizzling love scenes, and brilliant, imaginative worldbuilding, The Dante's Circle series reads as if Carrie Ann Ryan peeked at my personal wish list!" – NYT Bestselling Author, Larissa Ione

"Carrie Ann Ryan writes sexy shifters in a world full of passionate happily-ever-afters." – *New York Times* Bestselling Author Vivian Arend

"Carrie Ann's books are sexy with characters you can't help but love from page one. They are heat and heart blended to perfection." *New York Times* Bestselling Author Jayne Rylon

Carrie Ann Ryan's books are wickedly funny and deliciously hot, with plenty of twists to keep you guessing. They'll keep you up all night!" USA Today Bestselling Author Cari Quinn

"Once again, Carrie Ann Ryan knocks the Dante's Circle series out of the park. The queen of hot, sexy, enthralling paranormal romance, Carrie Ann is an author not to miss!" *New York Times* bestselling Author Marie Harte

Chapter One

Archer

Finding yourself when you previously thought you knew who you were isn't uncomplicated. Or perhaps is an instrumental challenge. Using the phrase "finding yourself" when all you wanted to do was look towards the future and pretend you hadn't had a breakdown of some sort didn't make much sense to me.

So, now I stood in front of a home that wasn't mine, that could be, and wondered exactly how I had gotten myself into this situation.

"Thank you so much for going through everything with us, I know that this isn't your normal expertise, but we're excited."

I looked over at Evelyn and Robert and grinned. "No problem. I'm going to enjoy doing this. It's not often that I get to work wood with my hands."

Neither one of them blinked, and I hadn't actually meant for the innuendo, but now I had to keep from snorting like a teenage boy.

Or maybe just like a Montgomery.

Marc had always hated when I made inappropriate jokes. Never at inappropriate times. I wasn't an idiot. I knew when I could snort to make dick jokes with my friends and family. This moment wasn't the time for it, so I didn't.

However, Marc had hated it at all times. He had never shamed me for it per se. But he had always looked down at me slightly for it. And cringed because that wasn't how he was.

I wasn't how he was.

We hadn't fit, and I hadn't realized it until it was too late.

And there was no going back to that time.

Marc was my ex-husband.

I didn't get to go back to that time and try to stand up for myself more, or pretend that I hadn't made one of the biggest mistakes of my life by not seeing each other for who we were.

"We're glad that we're hiring you. I know that we're working with Montgomery Builders, and you're coming out here as your side project, so your siblings are all welcome here as well as anyone you put on your staff. It'll be wonderful to see what you do. Since our views align so well."

I shook myself out of my reverie and looked back to Evelyn and Robert, who stood there, smiles on their faces and a slight sadness echoing in their eyes.

After all, they had lived in this cabin in the woods of the Rocky Mountains for years. They had raised their children here, had seen their first grandchildren here. Now, they wanted to move closer to Denver to be near those grandbabies. And with fires, weather, snow, ice, and the constant maintenance that came with a place like this, they wanted a change.

As I was living my change, I understood that all too well.

"Well, as you know, my sister is helping me with some of the designs, as she's a brilliant architect. Us working together on this is going to be great."

"I sure think so," Robert put in. "We're a good team, the three of us."

Evelyn smiled. "And while we're going to miss this place, we know that in the end, it's going to look even better than when we had it and go to a wonderful family."

My heart twinged at that because I wanted this house. It seemed kind of awkward, wanting a place that was out of my wheelhouse and not even up for sale yet. I needed to stop worrying about what I didn't have, and focus on what I did.

A job, siblings, parents, and nieces and nephews who loved me. A beautiful place to work, and good health. I had all of that. I just needed to focus on it a bit more.

"Anyway, we'll leave you to it. We have to head down to Denver now to go see our daughter." She beamed. "She'll be having our new grandson any day now, and we want to stay down there with her."

My heart warmed at that, and I couldn't stop grinning. "This is number four for you, then?" I asked, trying to remember.

"It is. Fourth grandson, sixth grandchild altogether. We can't wait." She looked up at her husband and as he smiled down at her, love shining in his eyes that I knew was just as intense if not more as it had been in the decades that they'd been together, I couldn't help but feel just a little bit of melancholy.

I would have that again. Or I wouldn't. I would be the best guncle there was out there.

"Are you staying with your daughter?" I asked, interested. I liked this couple and enjoyed the family stories.

They shook their heads in unison. "No, we're staying with our son. He lives nearby. We will be moving into our home in the neighborhood, one that your cousins built," she added with a wink.

I couldn't help but laugh. Montgomery Inc., down in Denver, was our sister company. It was always funny to me that both sets of cousins opened up construction companies and contracting.

We worked in the Fort Collins and Boulder areas, and they worked down in Denver and Colorado Springs.

I liked what they did; they were terrific. And, after many

years of my father hating them, it was nice that everyone was getting along again. We could hand over recommendations to anyone outside of our usual space.

"Are you moving in soon?" I asked.

"Next month. Most of our things are in storage now, but we stay here occasionally. But I do believe we have now spent our last night in this home." She looked up at the place, slid her hand into her husband's, and both of them leaned into each other, sighing.

I stood in silence, giving them some space. I didn't want to encroach, but I liked the fact that I could at least be on the periphery of this, to see the love and family that came after time. I was good at that, living on the fringe. But, it wasn't a place that I was entirely used to.

After a while, we said our goodbyes, and I went to my notes, looking through everything that I had to do.

I was the master plumber for Montgomery Builders. I had a full team that helped me with all of the plumbing for every new build or restoration that we did. We worked on neighborhoods, corporate buildings, and unique pieces. We didn't do full restorations of cabins like this often, only when something special came along. And this one was special.

They wanted to restore it to its former glory, as well as adding a few modern touches, and it just so happened that every single thing that they wanted in it for the sale was exactly what I would have done.

I wanted this house, but it didn't make much sense. I

had a beautiful apartment that I loved in Fort Collins, over an hour away. It wouldn't make much sense for me to have a place here, too. And yet, this place called to me.

That was probably another reason I was working on it alone rather than asking my family to help. After all, my family consisted of architects, actual builders, electricians—everything that you could ever imagine.

And I was the plumber.

I knew how to do nearly everything that my siblings could do, and what I couldn't for this project, they would help in an instant. We all had our own individual projects; we didn't work on every single thing together. It made for a healthy family and business.

I wanted to make my mark on this place, even if I wasn't the one that was going to end up living here.

A car pulled up after Evelyn and Robert left, and I turned to see my twin sister driving, and a familiar face in the passenger's seat.

I knew that my twin Annabelle was here because this was a Montgomery project, and she had every right to be here. After all, she had helped me with all the designs since she was a brilliant architect. But she was also here to check on me. Yes, everybody was worried about Archer. That wasn't something I was necessarily used to, yet I couldn't walk away from it.

"Oh good, you're here."

I rolled my eyes. "You knew I was going to be here."

"Well, I'm glad you're still here. You don't have cell service right now."

I cringed and looked down at my phone. "It seems not. One of the mudslides from last week knocked out a tower, and everything's a little spotty right now."

"I don't know how you people can stand being so rural out here. I'm attached to my phone at all times."

"Well, you're a businesswoman, a mother of two, and constantly addicted to the internet. It only makes sense."

I held out my arms, and my twin wrapped her arms around my waist and hugged me tightly. I did the same to her, shuddering a bit despite wanting to be strong.

My sister looked like me, with deep blue eyes, with her long flowing brown hair tied up behind her today. My hair was getting a little long, though hers had always had a slight wave to it. Maybe if I let my hair grow out, that wave would show up.

We were twins and looked enough alike that most people knew we were siblings right away. That was the case with all of our siblings.

Annabelle was shorter than me by a few inches, but I didn't tower over her too much. Probably because while my shoulders were broad, I was on the slender side. Annabelle was a little curvier, and our brothers were far more muscular. Our little sister, Paige, was smaller than Annabelle but full of way more energy. The fact that Paige was now a mom, and our brothers Benjamin and Beckett were parents as well, meant that I rarely got to see them as much as I used to. Even our board meetings had to be digital these days unless something was super important and we had to meet in person. We were on individual projects or working from home. Montgomery Builders had put in an entire childcare facility in our expansion. That way, anybody that worked for us could have childcare without having to have an additional expense or worry about it in the slightest. But sometimes, they wanted to work from home or bring the kids with them to the job sites. At least when it was safe to do so.

Everybody was growing up and moving on, and I loved them for it. I loved the expansion of our family and how our business was booming, to the point where we had to turn down jobs or change the way we were doing things with our larger teams.

Only, it still felt like I was holding on to this one project far harder than I should because I needed it to be mine.

"Well, I'm glad I'm here because this project of yours is going to be amazing." She kissed my chin and moved back, so Leif could step forward.

My nephew surprised me because he did not look like he could be our nephew. The kid wasn't a kid anymore—he was now in his twenties and in art school. His nearly black hair was pulled back in a small ponytail, his eyes blue and piercing, and he grinned at us, looking like a man instead of the little kid that I had once known.

He had some ink on him, and I knew one day, if he followed in his father's footsteps, he might just end up doing more ink on his own.

Technically, he wasn't my nephew. He was my cousin, Austin Montgomery's, son. Leif was the oldest of his cousins, like his father, Austin. I was on the younger end of all the cousins. All of my siblings were just now having babies, and Leif was out here, an adult in his own right, taking over the world.

I just shook my head, looking at the kid that was no longer a kid.

"I didn't know you were going to be here." I held up my arms again. Leif gave me a hard hug, then moved back. That's what I loved about the Montgomerys. We always hugged. No matter what. Because we were family, it didn't matter who was watching.

"I'm shadowing Annabelle today. She's a brilliant artist, though she just calls it math and architecture." Leif rolled his eyes.

I grinned. "Are you going to shadow me soon then?"

I wasn't expecting an answer, but Leif grinned, nodding quickly.

"I will. Paige is next week because I want to learn the ins and outs there, but I'm having fun shadowing as many people as I can. I'm learning as much as I can, all while in art school."

"So you can figure out what you want to be when you grow up," Annabelle added as she put her arm around his waist. He towered over her, looking like an actual adult, and it still startled me.

"I am a grown-up now. Watch out." He grinned as he said it, the ring in his brow shining in the light.

I remember when I had had an eyebrow ring, had been about his age. Maybe I should do it again. I wasn't that old. Hell, I was closer to Leif's age than I was to Austin's. I wasn't hitting my dotage yet.

"Anyway, we're out here because we wanted to see if you needed anything and because I wanted to check on you."

I snorted at my twin. "Not subtle at all, are you?"

"I don't have to be subtle. I'm Annabelle Montgomery-Queen. I can just be blunt."

I snorted. "I get it. So, what are you checking on me for?" I asked, far more cautiously than I used to. Annabelle must have heard it in my voice but just smiled at me.

"Honestly, because I couldn't get ahold of you, I wanted to make sure that you were okay."

"I'm fine. You knew I was going to be out here."

"And since there was no service, I worried. Sue me." I leaned forward, kissed her on the top of the head, and Leif just shook his head.

"I know she also wants to go over architecture things for you, but she has another thing to say."

Annabelle glared up at him. "Narc."

Leif raised a brow. "You should just get it over with."

Dread settled over me. "What is it? Is it the kids?"

"The kids are fine," she whispered quickly. "Hailey and Jack are just hanging out with Mom and Dad today. They wanted grandparent day."

I smiled at the thought of my niece and nephew. They were adorable. Little twin terrors, but then again, Annabelle and I had been the same way. We were our parents' second set of twins. Beckett and Benjamin are older than us. Paige is the baby of the family and had always wanted to be a twin, though I don't know what my family would have done if we'd had a third set of twins. Annabelle was the only one of us kids with twins so far, but there was always time.

It still startled me to think about everybody being parents now, while I was a divorced gay man working my ass off on projects that I should probably ask for help with more.

But there was no going back. And I needed to remember that.

"What is it then?" I asked, wondering why she was here.

"If you're willing, I want to set you up on a blind date."

I froze, alarm hitting me. "Annabelle, no."

"It's been a year, Archer. Let us have fun. You'll like him. He's a social media consultant that I know."

I rolled my eyes. "I do not need to date a social media consultant. I know you love the internet, but as you can see, I'm doing just fine out here with no service."

She narrowed her eyes at me. "You're the one that taught us all about doing videos dancing for social media. And all the different trends. And now you're saying you don't want to know a social media consultant?"

"I'm saying that I don't need to be set up on a blind

date. I could go on a date if I wanted to. I'm not a decrepit old man hiding in the shadows."

No, I was just a feeble man hiding in the shadows. One that felt old. But I didn't say that part out loud.

"I'm not doing the blind date thing."

"You should," Leif said.

I narrowed my eyes at the kid. "Excuse me?"

"What? If you don't want the social media operator, then I know a few people. Models." He raised his brows, and I groaned.

"When did you get old enough to have model friends?"

"I'm just saying they're pretty hot."

"And have you slept with any of them?" I asked, narrowing my eyes.

Annabelle coughed. "You can't ask that."

"Hey, I don't want anyone that my younger second-cousin has slept with."

"We're nearly the same age. It might just happen."

"I don't know. That's not something that I need to worry about."

"What? We're both bisexual. It might just happen if we hang out in the same places." Leif just grinned, and I pinched the bridge of my nose.

"I hate you. I'm not going to go on a blind date. I love you both. I love all of my family. But I'm not going to go on blind dates."

"Then you should find a date for yourself," Annabelle said softly.

"I don't know. If it happens, it happens. But I'm busy. Hell, you are too. I'm surprised you had time to come out here."

"I always have time for you." She leaned forward, kissed me on the cheek, hugged me tightly, and when she and Leif left, after going over a few things for the project, I stood at the home that I wanted to be mine but knew it made no sense, and got to work.

The plumbing would have to be rehauled entirely to get up to the new codes, and we wanted to add more environmentally friendly aspects to the place. It would sell as soon as it went on the market. It was a great location and very sought after, and I knew that Evelyn and Robert already had a few people biting.

It was sad that I kind of wanted it to be me.

First, though, I had to go onto the roof and check a few things. I pulled out the ladder, rolled my shoulders back, and climbed up.

Today was a nice day, the sun shining through the Rockies and the giant trees around us. It hadn't rained in over two months, and that was slightly worrying, but hopefully it would soon. We did live in a desert, even though we were against the Rockies. It just didn't feel like that all the time, not with the green foliage.

I walked across the flat part of the roof, taking mental notes of things I would need to update or go through. The roof didn't need to be completely redone, but there were some places I wanted to double-check.

Something moved out of the corner of my eye, and I turned to see a man in flannel, worn jeans, and dirty-blond hair walking along a path. I knew there was another house back there, from what Evelyn and Robert had said, but I hadn't seen him before.

I couldn't see his face, but his muscular build, broad shoulders, and very tight ass in those jeans had me swallowing hard.

Well, hell. I hadn't had that kind of interest in a while.

I shook my head and then got back to work.

By the time I was done, all thoughts of the sexy blond man were out of my head, and the sheer immensity of things on my to-do list, let alone everything that I had to do for Montgomery Builders, was starting to weigh on me.

I took a step down onto the ladder, not looking, and reached out for the edge of the awning as the ladder twisted, somehow sliding off the rocks below.

I shouted, my pulse racing, as I reached for the gutter, and as it snapped under my hands, fragments of my life flashing before my eyes as I hoped to hell that whatever I fell on below wouldn't kill me right away.

The ground came up far too quickly, and I screamed.

Chapter Two

Killian

The impact knocked the breath out of me and I fell back, slamming into the pile of leaves behind me. The slender man in my arms let out an 'oof', as well, as he splayed on top of me, thigh against thigh, leg against leg, and chest against chest. There were probably other things pressing against one another, but all I could do was hold my breath. I wondered why the hell I'd even rushed over here.

The man was breathing. I could tell that much from the raspy noises above me, and I didn't think I'd broken anything on my end. Other than perhaps my dignity.

After all, I had rushed over with my arms out as a man

fell off his damn roof, and here I was, shaking, pretending I knew what the fuck I was doing.

Of course, that seemed like what I usually did these days. *Pretend*.

"Oh my God."

The man had a pleasant voice. I could tell that much, at least. It didn't sound broken. Maybe I was; I didn't know at this point.

"What the hell?" he asked as he rolled off of me. I groaned, letting out a curse as the man's elbow got me right in the gut, and the man with dark hair, piercing blue eyes, and a blank expression stared at me.

"Did I crush you? You caught me. I just fell off a fucking roof."

I lay there in the leaves, wanting to be anywhere but here, and looked over at the man.

"Why the hell did you put your ladder on those fucking rocks? You were just asking to fall."

The other man blinked slowly, then looked down at the fallen ladder and then at me. "I'm sorry. You saved me."

Those words were like throwing ice on me, and I slowly sat up, checking myself for injuries, grateful to not see any blood or a random bone sticking out.

"I just helped move you towards the leaves that would've caught your fall anyway. Didn't have anything to do with it." My voice was gruff, a little raspy. Considering I only spoke with Penny these days, it made sense. Talking to myself in the darkness didn't count as conversation either.

"Oh. Well. Thank you. Seriously. And the ladder was secure. I swear. I'm a professional."

I looked him up and down and snorted. "Sure." I didn't know what kind of "professional" he was talking about, but calling him a prostitute when I was in a fucking bad mood and knowing I would be bruised and achy all over later didn't sound like something I should be saying. I was learning not to be an asshole.

The other man stiffened in front of me before he raised his chin and glared. "Yes. I'm an owner of Montgomery Builders. I'm their plumber and know what the fuck I'm doing."

"Since when is plumbing on the roof?" I asked, wondering why the hell I kept needling him. I didn't care. This man had nothing to do with me. Other than the fact that I had just been his landing pad for his incompetence.

"I'm more than just a plumber. Not that there's anything *just* about being a plumber," the other man snarled, his cheeks reddening.

"Fine. I'm not going to judge you for your work. Because, hell, I don't care."

"You sure sound a bit judgy," he singsonged, and I just sighed.

"You just landed on me, with the force of however many pounds you are. Sorry for not being in a good mood."

The other man paled again, looked up at the roof, and sighed. "I'm sorry. You're right. I was just scared. I am grateful. I'm Archer Montgomery."

He held out his hand, and I looked down at it as if some part of me was trying to remember what I was supposed to do with that.

His face fell again, and I cleared my throat and decided that they wouldn't have wanted me to be an asshole.

I gripped his hand, shook it once before letting go quickly. I ignored the heat in it, the roughness of his palms. He did work with his hands, apparently. Maybe he was good at his job, just not great at ladders.

"Killian."

"Cool name," he said softly, and I shrugged.

They had always liked my name too.

"Well, I've always had it. So, I guess it is. You're not hurt, are you? Because I don't want to have to carry you down the mountain."

"I'm fine. Plus, you wouldn't have to carry me. There are vehicles."

"I'd have to carry you to the vehicle and get you down there. It's not like ambulances like to come up here."

"We're not that much in the wilderness," he said as he picked with a new hole on his jean knee. And that's when I realized we were both still sitting on the ground. I stood up quickly, ignoring the aches and pains in my lower back. Oh, I hadn't twinged something or broken anything, but I was going to be sore in the morning. Hell, I would be sore in the next ten minutes, and it would last for eons.

"Emergency services can get up here, but it's a lot of resources and a lot of time on their end. You're pretty much out on your own, especially since the cell tower's been down for so long."

"I noticed that. My sister came out to check on me because of it."

"Ah. That was that car."

"Spying, are you?" he asked, and I heard the teasing glint in his tone as he stood up and stretched, wincing a bit. I sighed, wondering why the hell I was even trying. I didn't try. That was the whole point.

"I don't honestly care. I have to get back to work. Did you buy the house from the previous owner? Are you just working?"

Archer frowned, probably wondering why I was such an asshole. There wasn't much left to wonder. I was just kind of an asshole.

"I'm fixing it up for them, our whole company is. But I don't know. It's a good place."

I looked at the nearly worn-down cabin and thought about the home that was worse off behind those trees. The place I spent every day pretending that I knew what the fuck I was doing.

"Well, there's nothing much up here. Don't know why you'd want to move out here." I shrugged. "If you're doing okay, I'm going to head out. Call down the mountain for help. Maybe a bear will come out and help you if you need it."

And with that, I turned on my heel and left while I felt Archer's glare on me.

The man seemed fine, he wasn't hurt, and I just needed to get back to the cabin. I had shit to do, a life to pretend I lived, and I didn't need to think about Archer fucking Montgomery.

"Thank you!" Archer yelled from behind me. I tensed but didn't turn back. "Seriously. The joy of your conversation has made this whole falling from a roof thing completely thrilling. I truly appreciate it."

I scowled, ignoring the way that my lips wanted to twitch. This was not funny. I did not find this guy funny. He was annoying. He was intruding on my solitude. That was the one thing I had, the one thing I was going to keep. So screw this.

I waved him off and ignored Archer muttering behind me and the sound of metal scraping against stone as he presumably picked up the ladder.

I wanted to stop what I was doing, go back and hold the damn thing for him, or tell him to get off the roof, but it wasn't my job. It wasn't my role. I didn't have any right to make sure that he was safe.

A bark sounded in front of me, and I leaned down and ran my hand over the yellow Lab's head. "Okay, Cora. Let's get back to work." She barked up at me, that doggy grin killing me.

Ecstatic about me just being around, she huffed and jumped and barked before carefully coming to my side and following me to the backside of the house. Her enthusiasm broke my heart, even as it made me smile. I wasn't very good at raising Cora. I was trying, but I knew who'd have been better at it. I pushed those thoughts from my mind and went back to work.

I was rebuilding this cabin from scratch, doing the one thing I had been good at before my life changed. It was odd to think that someone else had a whole business doing what I needed and was working next door. And since I could do the electrical but not the plumbing as well as I'd like, maybe I could ask Archer for help. Or hire him. But no, that was an idiotic thing to think. I had one thing to do. Take care of this house. And do what I should have done in the first place.

The first thing I needed to do, though, was prep for winter, which meant firewood. There were a few downed trees in the last storm, so I went to work. I'd been working on them since the storm, but with this many trees, it took months on top of all of my other work. I rolled up my flannel sleeves, pushed back my hair slightly, remembered it was in a ponytail, cursed at myself, and ignored it. Then I went to work. I set the log on the chopping block, swung, split it in two, and did it over and over again until the aching in my body from the fall burned but meant something. I felt something because of it, so I leaned into it, craving it.

I kept going, sweat slicking into my flannel, down my jeans, and over my face. I kept going until I couldn't hold the ax any longer, my hands aching, my gloves pushing new blisters onto my skin.

I set down the ax, careful not to startle Cora who napped behind me, and went back for my jug of water.

My phone buzzed in my back pocket, and I cursed. Sadly the damn thing hadn't broken in the fall, and it seemed that the cell tower was back up and running. Well, at least Archer's sister wouldn't be worried about him anymore.

I looked down at my phone and I sighed. But *my* sister was.

I thought about letting it go to voicemail like I usually did, but then she might come up here. And her drive was from Texas. She had moved down to the panhandle when her husband had been stationed at Dyess Air Force base in Abilene, and that wasn't an easy drive to check up on her dumbass brother.

I finally answered on the second to last ring and sighed. "Ann."

"You're alive." I heard the relief in her voice but forced myself to ignore it. "That's always good to know."

"Of course I am. And here, aren't I?"

"I wonder where *here* is." She sighed again, and I heard the pain in her tone. She was worried about me.

Hell, I didn't blame her, and yet I didn't care. I wanted to care, but it was hard to do so, not when the numbness that I was so used to was settling in again. It had vanished briefly after everything that had happened with Archer. But there was no going back now—no changing this. So I ignored it. It's what I was good at.

"Killian. You need to answer your phone."

"The cell tower was out. It's not like I purposely ignored you." *This time.*

"I don't like the idea that the phone was off and you couldn't get a hold of anyone. What if there was an emergency? What if you fell off that roof that you're building?"

This time my lips did quirk, the action stiff, different. If my sister only knew who had fallen off the roof.

"I'm fine, Ann. Cora and I are just working." At the sound of her name, Cora let out one good bark, that doggy grin coming back, and my sister sighed into the phone.

"Is she okay? We miss the both of you."

"I know you do, squirt."

"I am a mother of two and a wife. Please stop calling me squirt." She paused. "Scratch that. Call me squirt all you want. Just *call* me."

"I'm okay, Ann. I'm just working."

"You're not. You're scaring me, Killian. It's been three years. You're allowed to breathe."

Anger soared through me and I wanted to yell, curse at my sister, but that wasn't fair to her, and I didn't hurt my baby sister. No matter that she was my only family left other than Cora. But she had a family of her own. She was making a family of her own. I didn't need to be part of that, but I also didn't need to be cruel to her. I've already been an asshole to someone today. That should be my quota.

"Cora and I are doing just fine. I'm building. Working. Getting ready for winter."

"Will you come down for birthdays? Holidays? Can we come up to you? I know you say the cabin's not ready, but we can rent another one, get a hotel. I don't know...camp? Just let us."

"Ann." My body hurt, and not just from the fall. "I need time."

Ann was silent so long that I was afraid the tower had fallen again and we had lost our connection. "Okay. I'm going to tell you that you have all the time you need. It's just, I don't know how much time you want. I love you, Killian."

I closed my eyes, the pain slashing through my heart once again as if a thousand shards of glass were cascading through my soul. "I know."

I tried to say it back, but there was nothing left in me, and I hoped to hell my sister understood that. When she finally hung up after a moment of silence, I put my phone in my back pocket.

I looked down at Cora.

"I keep fucking up."

She tilted her head at me, her face so expressive.

"I'm trying."

Cora didn't say anything back, and so I sighed and went to clean up my mess.

"I brought cookies."

I whirled as Cora barked, then ran over to the one person who thought that they could walk on my property without a care in the world.

Of course, Penny could do whatever the hell she wanted. She was either in her forties, fifties, sixties, or nineties. I wasn't sure. She was a hippie, Boulder born and bred, and not always in her right mind. At least, that's what she liked to pretend.

And she had made me her pet project. So I didn't get a say about when she made her appearances. I had to put up with her whenever the hell she wanted. Then again, I got cookies out of the deal, so maybe this wasn't all that bad.

"Something is going on with you, honey."

"You say that every time you show up."

"And every time, I'm not shitting you. Now, I brought cookies for you, cookies for Cora, and you're going to go into that rat-ass kitchen of yours that you're still building and feed me."

My lips twitched, this time for real. Penny could do that.

And so, apparently, could Archer.

I ignored that thought, shook my head, and walked inside behind Penny, letting her lead the way.

"What happened in here?" she asked as she looked at the mess all over my kitchen.

I froze, cursing under my breath. "Those fucking raccoons."

"In the day?" Worry etched her tone.

"Or it's an opossum. Or a deer, I don't know. Something keeps getting into my shit and fucking things up."

There were broken plates on the floor, little paw footprints that looked like a raccoon, trash spilled everywhere, and just a mess.

"If I didn't know any better, I'd say that crew of raccoons are out to get you."

I scowled. "They are. Look at this mess."

"I'll help you clean it up. You're going to have to bleach this. You don't need bears stumbling in."

I shuddered. "That momma bear and her three cubs sure do love visiting. At least they did last season."

Penny smiled up at me. "Well, we'll clean this up, eat some cookies, and you can tell me why you're limping."

I hadn't even realized I had been, my leg didn't hurt, but my hip was aching.

"A man fell on top of me."

Penny grinned, her eyes going bright. "What kind of man? I wish a man would fall on top of me."

I rolled my eyes. Even though she was a self-declared hippie and all about free love, Penny had been married for forty years and lost her husband five years ago. She hadn't even been on a date or thought about another man, other than Chris Evans, since. Her screwing with me like this was just her.

"He fell off a roof. I caught him. And now I hurt."

Her gaze went straight to worry. "Is he okay? Is it that new one, the hot hunky one with a nice ass that's helping rebuild Evelyn and Robert's house?"

I rolled my eyes. "Of course, you know that man."

"I see that you haven't said he doesn't have a nice ass."

"Well, I'm not going to lie to you, Penny."

"My God," she said, staggering back. "Was that a joke? That didn't have cursing? I just...I think I need to sit down. Eat some cookies. Only I think there's trash on the seat so let's clean this up, and then you can regale me with tales of this man that fell right on top of you, all sexy and swoony."

I scowled. "He fell off a roof because he's a fucking idiot. I don't think that's sexy."

"I can make my own story up then."

I shook my head and helped Penny clean up my kitchen, wondering what the fuck I had done to those raccoons and why they had it out for me.

And I didn't think about Archer Montgomery, or that nice ass of his, at all.

Chapter Three

Archer

I pinched the bridge of my nose, angry with myself for getting into this situation. My body hurt, my head ached, and the paperwork in front of me just wasn't going away anytime soon.

I had been putting off a lot of paperwork that my sister needed for the past month or so. It wasn't that I wasn't good at the paperwork. I was. I just hadn't been in the mood. That was something very much unlike me, but now I didn't have a choice. Paige needed these final invoices and any labor that I had used. In addition, I needed to work on the initial receipts and project plans for the house up on the mountain.

My sister was our administrative assistant, although really, she was the one who ran the whole place so we could all focus.

We couldn't run this business without her because she was our boss, just without the title. Although I often called her boss to her face, and she enjoyed it. Along with our accountant, she worked things so that I didn't have to worry about the management aspects of this job most of the time. I could be a plumber, do the planning on all of the pipes and layouts for the new houses—and renovations, as was the case of the cabin in the woods.

Beckett would come eventually and help me with the general contracting because that's what he was good at, and anything I couldn't do myself, he or his team would do. I just wanted to see how much of it I could do myself first. Because it felt like this was mine, even though it wasn't on the market yet, and I hadn't put in an offer. Not that I would put in an offer. Because it was far away, and that would be silly. Wouldn't it?

Benjamin was our landscape architect and had even won awards recently. He had waved them off, calling it silly, but he was brilliant at what he did.

I was just grateful that he would help with whatever I couldn't do later.

Annabelle had already done a lot of work to design the new elements. The team and I were going to incorporate as much as we could, so that way this place felt a little bit like mine, and saying goodbye to it after I was done was going to suck.

I was getting better at saying goodbye, wasn't I?

At that thought, I rolled my eyes, annoyed with myself

for being so damn emotional and whiny. Just because I was divorced, slightly unhappy, and living alone as the rest of my family got married and had kids and moved on without me didn't make me a sad case. I needed to remember what I cherished in life. What I had that was good. I just wanted to be a little whiny today.

"Are you coming to Riggs' tonight?" Paige asked as she walked in, her hair in a perfect updo on the top of her head, her bright blue eyes slightly full of worry, because everyone was worried about me.

Odd to think, since I used to be the one worried about Paige. However, my baby sister was all grown up, a mother herself, and didn't have the issues that she once had.

I was the one messing up even when I wasn't trying.

"I don't know if I want to go to Riggs'," I said after a moment.

Paige's brows shot up, and I held back a curse. "You're not going to come with us tonight?"

Riggs' was our favorite bar and grill that also happened to have a dancing hall. It was slightly Western, slightly contemporary, and just fun.

It was also owned by a friend of ours, Riggs, and his husband Clay. Clay worked for us and had once been Beckett's trainee and assistant project manager, but now was a construction lead all on his own. He ran crews under Beckett, but only because Beckett was the main boss. After a few years of working hard, Clay now could own his own company if he wanted to. He liked working with the Montgomerys, and we enjoyed having him here. Our family was growing, as was our business. And that meant we had people without the Montgomery name in lead positions. A far cry from our parents, but I liked it. Clay was practically part of the family. His three kids called my parents grandma and grandpa at this point.

The bar that Riggs owned, and now Clay too thanks to their marriage, was our local watering hole. We used to go there once a week, usually on Thursdays, since it wouldn't be as busy, and we would hang out, dance, maybe have a drink or two, and just enjoy ourselves as a family.

Then, one by one, everybody started getting married— including me. All of us got married, and the others began having kids. So even though sometimes they went while pregnant or left the babies at home, the once-a-week dinners at Riggs' turned into twice a month. Sometimes it was once a month if we were busy. Because, in addition to our time at Riggs', we also had family dinners that we alternated around each of the family's homes.

Not mine in a while, though, because it had never worked out. Marc usually had to work at his high-powered job and it had always been weird hosting a dinner when my husband couldn't be there. And, frankly, we were loud. All us Montgomerys in one place made a lot of noise and scared people away.

So we tended to be at everybody else's homes, including my parents. Now though, while I didn't have Marc saying no, I also didn't have the space. I lived in a small apartment, trying to figure out what house I would move into. Because I had sold the home I had bought on my own when I had married Marc. Marc's had been closer to the middle between both of our workplaces, so it made sense, and I had liked Marc's contemporary home. It was gorgeous, with clean lines, an architectural masterpiece. One not built by a Montgomery, but it'd been amazing. But now I didn't know what I wanted to do. I needed to either buy a condo, build a house here, buy a house we'd already built, or maybe, do something a little different. Drastic.

Like move to the mountains, and figure out what to do. But over an hour of driving back and forth just to work seemed like an idiotic thing to do.

Unless we were serious about opening up the Boulder branch.

I pushed that thought out of my head. "I've just had a long day. I'm tired," I said, not lying to my sister.

She studied my face and sighed. "I just don't know when we're going to be able to go to Riggs' again with all of us. I know you and the guys tend to try to do things together. I thought it would be nice to have all of us."

"Okay." I knew she was guilting me, but not on purpose. I wanted to spend time with my family, but I still felt off.

"Now I feel horrible," she said after a minute, and I blinked.

"You feel horrible that I'm going?" I asked, laughing.

"No, because now I feel like I pushed you into it."

I stood up and held out my arms. My baby sister came to me, wrapped her arms around my waist, and sighed.

"I feel like I never get to see you."

I kissed the top of her head and held her tightly, ignoring the fact that my sides hurt where she was touching. It wasn't her fault. She didn't know that I had fallen off a roof yesterday. I was fine, but I still ached, not to mention the huge bruise that I had that I would have to hide from everybody else. I didn't want them to worry about me. They had been worrying about me forever, and I didn't need to add to it. Added to the fact that I didn't want them to think I couldn't handle this job on my own. While a certified plumber, I also had the skills necessary to do nearly everything but some electric.

I had been learning my entire life how to be a general contractor and, while I wasn't the architect that Annabelle was, I was still good at most things.

"Come on. We'll go tonight. Have fun, and I get to see all of my siblings. Are the spouses going?"

"Yes. But you're family. You're not a ninth wheel."

I winced. "That's lovely. I wasn't even thinking I was going to be a ninth wheel. At that point, am I just a part of a bus?" I rubbed the spot over my heart, almost playing along.

"That's not what I meant. I'm just not saying the right things around you. This is why we need to spend more time together."

"But I like going over to your houses to see you guys. To see Emery."

Paige beamed at the thought of her baby, and I just shook my head.

"You see? Between Rafael, Lexington, Hailey, Jack, and now Emery, I'm full of nieces and nephews. I like us doing the quieter meals at home where I can spend time with the babies."

"And we have babysitters tonight, and Clay got babysitters too. So he will be there with Riggs, who promises to come out and dance with us."

"That makes me an eleventh wheel, Paige," I murmured, and she winced.

"What about that guy that Annabelle said she was going to hook you up with?"

My body tensed. "Hook up? Is that what you're going with?"

"Oh, shut up. I don't know. We know that my dating life was not great until Lee."

"Did you and Lee even date? Or did you guys just accidentally get married?"

"Some things were accidental, and it wasn't the marriage," she teased, and I groaned.

"I do not need to think about those things."

"True."

"Okay, I will go. I will dance. I'm not going to be set up or hooked up with anybody. I'm just going to have fun with you guys."

"That's all we want. Because we love you."

The way she said that told me that they had once again been talking about me.

Because they were worried about their brother.

I did not want to be their worry anymore. I wanted to be the guy who knew what he was doing and didn't make people feel as if they had to tiptoe around him.

"We'll go dancing. Have fun. And maybe I'll hook up with some random guy there."

"You know, that's one of those things you should not tell your baby sister, but if hooking up with somebody—rather than dating them—makes you happy, go for it. Because all I want for you is to be happy."

I shook my head and smiled and then pushed her gently out of my office so I could get back to work.

That was the problem with the fact that everybody I knew was married. They all had families and were ready to spend the rest of their lives together. They clearly wanted to make sure that everyone else in their lives was happy and settled as well.

I had been happy and settled. Okay, in retrospect, I had been settled.

Marc hadn't been for me. He had been slightly controlling but not mean about it. Not exactly. He hadn't hurt me, except my pride and my heart. He hadn't been the one for me, and we had made mistakes.

I wasn't going to make those mistakes again.

I didn't need a husband, or even a boyfriend. All I needed was to figure out my place and to see exactly why I once again felt as if I were putting myself in a box I didn't need to be.

I went back to work, and looked up in surprise as my dad stood there. He put his hands in his pockets, looking awkward, and I just smiled at him. My parents had never had an issue that I was gay. They hadn't even been surprised. The fact that most of my extended family was somewhere on the queer spectrum probably helped with that.

It had just been one more thing that made us family. They had supported me. Because not everybody outside our family had agreed with my sexuality, as if it was something for them to be in agreement with.

They had never made me feel anything less than loved, and had made sure that nobody treated me like I was worthless. When a teacher had been concerned that the high school quarterback and I were getting too close, my parents had politely told the teacher to fuck off.

My dad had been my advocate, except for when it came to my job. My dad had wanted me to be an electrician, or even follow in the same footsteps as Beckett. But I had wanted to be different. Maybe I was just going through issues, and I had wanted to be a plumber because no one else in the family was.

I was good at my job, but I still liked learning other skills. And, so, my dad and I had fought. It hadn't been because of who I was. No, it had been for the choices I had made because we couldn't see eye to eye.

But those days were in our past. And I was forever grateful that they were.

"You know I always hated the paperwork part of this job," Dad said as he came forward.

I leaned back into my chair and smiled up at him.

"Really?"

"Absolutely hated it. Your mom was always better at it. Of course, that always made me feel bad because I felt like I was putting your mom into that position."

"Mom would never let you put her into any position."

"That is true. My wife is pretty special."

And that right there was the reason why, no matter how many times Dad and I had fought over the years over his controlling tendencies with the company and my career, I'd always loved him.

"I know you guys are going to Riggs' tonight, and your mom and I are going out to dinner. I just wanted to stop by and say hello."

"I'm glad you're here."

"It's kind of nice hearing that, since I was such a jerk for so long; having you guys think it is nice that I'm here is pretty cool."

I winced. "It is nice that you're here," I whispered.

"Anyway, I was talking with Annabelle earlier about that project in the woods."

I sat up straighter. "Oh yeah?"

"Yes. I know you're doing most of it independently, and I applaud that. Hell, there were a couple of places that just felt like they needed to be mine and not the company's. I know that your siblings sometimes find that with certain pieces too. But not always."

I nodded. "Yeah, they don't always have the same ideas as me when it comes to what is a special project or not."

"Because you guys are all different. I'm sure there were certain projects that were closer to Annabelle than they were to you."

"True. I don't know what it is about it. This place just speaks to me."

My father looked at me then and nodded. "I know everybody is busy and working on a hundred different things since you guys are making this place shine, but if you ever need a set of hands up there, a quiet set of hands, call me. I'd love to help."

I froze, blinking. "Oh. That would be, you know, that would be pretty amazing. You're a lot better at electrical work than I am."

"I've kept up my credentials, too. I'm a certified electrician."

I grinned. "I am not. Just a certified plumber and contractor."

"And talented at both. The team will help, of course. But if you need more, I'm there."

I stood up then, moved around to hug my dad tight. He stiffened for just a moment, mostly because I had surprised him, and I hadn't hugged as many people recently as I should have, and he hugged me back.

"I love you, Archer."

For some reason, I held back tears as I swallowed hard. "I love you too, Dad."

My voice cracked, and I let out a huge sigh as we just stood there hugging, until my dad quietly patted my back, nodded tightly, and walked away.

I loved my parents. They loved each other and were good parents. Yes, they had had issues with the way that we had handled the company, but that had been on them, and we were past that. And I didn't know why I just wanted to cry right then.

* * *

At the end of the workday, I stretched my back, wincing at the pain. I knew I hadn't broken anything, but the huge bruise on my side ached, and all I wanted to do was take a hot bath in my tiny apartment and pretend that I hadn't made a fool out of myself in front of a hot guy.

I was getting good at making a fool of myself, wasn't I?

I picked up my things, and rather than heading home, used the large shower in my office to get ready. Since I had designed the plumbing in this place, I had made sure I had the best shower, considering my job.

I headed over to Riggs' after, knowing we would eat dinner there. Riggs' offered bar food and giant salads, and their food was just getting better and better as Riggs found his routine. By the time I got there, I happened to be the last one there. Everybody was there with all of their spouses, and I just smiled at my family.

Annabelle and Jacob were on the dance floor, Jacob holding his wife close enough that I held back a sigh. Brenna and Benjamin were at the bar, helping Riggs and Clay with a tray of drinks for the table. Eliza and Beckett were at the table, laughing with one another, as Paige and Lee sat in the booth next to them, the two tables pushed together with more chairs added to accommodate our big group.

Everybody looked happy, ready to hang out, so why did I feel like I was on the outside looking in?

Annabelle moved towards me and laughed as she ran and jumped. I held up my arms instinctively and caught her, letting out a groan as I did.

"What did I do? Did I hurt you? You've never groaned while catching me before." She moved back, her eyes wide, and as she pulled up the side of my shirt to see what had made me wince, she paled. "What the hell happened? Are you okay?"

And then everybody was there. Even strangers were looking at us.

I blushed, annoyed with myself.

"I had a little accident at work. I'm fine."

"An accident!" Paige exclaimed.

"I sort of fell off a roof."

"Sort of fell off a roof?" Beckett growled. "How do you *sort of* fall off a roof?"

"Because I wasn't really on top of the roof. Just on the ladder-ish. It's fine. The neighbor broke my fall."

Everybody was silent for a moment before they all talked at once, and I held up my hands.

"I need a fucking drink. I'm fine. I didn't break anything. And I didn't break the neighbor."

"Was the neighbor hot at least?" Lee asked, grinning at me.

I knew he was trying to cut the tension, and I would forever be grateful to my brother-in-law.

"He was okay," I said, completely lying.

"Oh, that means he was sexy as hell. Tell us more about this neighbor that you fell on top of," Eliza singsonged as she moved forward to pat my face gently. "Let's get you something to drink, and you can tell us all about this hunky man."

"I didn't say he was hunky," I grumbled as they pushed me towards the booth and put a beer in my hand.

I looked around at my family and reminded myself that I was happy. They made me happy. I didn't need more than this.

And I didn't need to think about a hunky blond man that I happened to know what it felt like to be pressed up against.

Chapter Four

Killian

Ice slicked along my skin, through my pores, up my throat and nose, and seeped out of my eyes. Everything was ice, a pure chill that would never go away. I choked myself awake as if I were still coughing up that icy water and swallowed hard, wiping away the damp sweat all over me.

Cora stood on top of me on the bed, her little Lab face full of worry.

I honestly didn't know if I would have woken up without reliving countless versions of the unending nightmare without her on top of me.

Cora barked once, loud and sharp, and I laughed. I couldn't help it.

"That's a good girl. I'm awake—no more nightmares."

She gave me a look like she clearly didn't believe me. I was awake, but we both knew the nightmares would come again.

I shook my head before I sat up and she got off of me, but instead of jumping off the bed, she scrambled off to the side of me, wanting a full belly rub. I obliged, loving how she still acted like a puppy even though she was four years old now, and everyone kept telling me that she would eventually calm down. But no, she was an outdoor dog who wanted to live on the posh side of bougieness when it came to this bedroom. Meaning she had her dog bed but slept in my bed. While I would have been fine with a cot, or even a sleeping bag on the floor, Cora needed something more. I got a king-sized bed with an adjustable base so she would always be comfortable, even during the nights where I couldn't sleep, paced outside, or went back to work. Cora was the one who got her sleep every night with the down comforter and soft sheets.

I hadn't had anyone in this bed other than the two of us, and since I didn't see that changing anytime soon, my dog got what she wanted.

When Cora rolled off the bed and went to the front of the house, I followed her, sliding on a pair of sweats as I did so. I always slept in at least underwear around her since I didn't need those doggy paws anywhere near certain parts of me, but I hated sleeping in anything else since I tended to twist and turn.

I let her out to do her business and then kept the door open so she could make her way back inside. She did so, somehow closing the door behind her. She was far too clever for this early in the morning.

"Thank you. Since the sun isn't up, I guess those raccoons could come back."

She gave me a patient look, and I just smiled.

"Okay, let's get some coffee and see what we're going to do for the day."

She looked at her bowl, and then her water dish, and gave me such a pleading look that I put my hand over my chest.

"I know. I'm starving you. How on earth are you supposed to make it through the day since you haven't had food since your snack at eight last night? It's four in the morning now. You must be starving."

She gave another bark and I smiled. With that rusty smile still in place, I went to feed her, give her water, and grabbed my cup of coffee once it finished brewing.

"Now, what are we going to do for the day? Want to go for a hike?"

She gave me a look before she returned to her breakfast, and I sighed.

"Okay, we did the hike yesterday. We could do it again, but I know we need to work on the project's next phase. I don't want to have to hire a damn plumber since the last one flaked out on us."

She licked the last of her bowl and then came up to me, putting her head on my knee.

I sighed. "I know I could ask the neighbor. Or I could just ask Penny. She would know someone."

Cora just blinked at me.

"Okay, so maybe knowing Penny, she would just tell me to use the neighbor since she knows everything, but it's fine. For all I know, Archer Montgomery quit his job because he fell off the roof, and Evelyn and Roger didn't want to deal with it anymore."

Cora let out a huff, then went to the back door, her butt wiggling.

"Let's go for a walk, and then we'll figure out what to do. You are very demanding."

She let out an indignant huff and I snorted before grabbing my shoes and her leash. Though I would walk her off-leash for a bit on our property, she'd be on leash as soon as we went off the property into the mountains. There were too many bears, other wildlife, and hikers around for me not to.

I frowned, looked at my phone for the date again, and nodded. It wasn't hunting season, so we wouldn't need her jacket, but soon it would be, then she'd need her little jacket so people would realize that she wasn't a deer or whatever the hell they wanted to hunt.

I shook my head and let Cora lead me around for a short walk, letting my thoughts rest.

The nightmare hadn't been that bad this time.

I didn't go more than a few days without a nightmare, but it sort of worried me that it had been long enough without such a bad one that I woke up throwing up or not able to sleep for a week.

My therapist would have said something helpful about that, but that would require me to go back to my therapist, and I wasn't really in the mood. That's why I had bought this damn place after all and had moved out here—to get away from it all.

I sighed, finished my coffee, and followed Cora back to the house. Apparently, we were on a schedule today that I was unaware of.

As soon as my door opened, my brows raised and I realized why Cora had been in such a hurry to get back to the house even when it was only six in the morning.

"There you are. I took the liberty of making myself some coffee."

I rolled my eyes at Penny. "Well then, make yourself at home."

"Of course, I did. I can do what I want. I'm old."

I moved past her and made myself a second cup. "Whatever. If you're going to call *yourself* old, I must be ancient."

"Of the soul and the body are two separate things, darling."

I ignored that pointed remark because she was right.

"You're telling me you went for such a long walk that you sweated through your top but only took a single mug of coffee?

"It was a large cup, and it was in a travel mug. It was enough."

"From those dark circles under your eyes, I think you're a liar."

"I'm fine. I'll drink water after this. And, who knows, maybe I'll even have a glass of whiskey with you later."

"I do love our whiskey nights, and a glass of pinot noir every once in a while."

"I only drink with you around, Penny. Don't worry. I'm a hermit, but not a completely self-destructive one."

"Cora doesn't think you're a hermit." She sipped her coffee, studying my face too clearly.

"What is it?" I asked with a sigh.

"How's your back from that fall?" she asked, reaching down to pet the top of Cora's head as she leaned heavily into the woman.

I shrugged, the pain fading. "It's been a few days. I'm fine. I didn't hit that hard, and the leaves were close enough."

"Not close enough to catch all of your fall. I'm glad you helped the neighbor, though. I met him yesterday."

My brows winged up. "You did?

"Offhandedly, I waved and welcomed him to the neighborhood, even though he said he was just building, before I headed off. I had a yoga class."

I wasn't sure where she was going with this, so I did my best to lead the conversation from any dangerous areas. "Now that you've met him, he can be your problem."

"I wasn't aware he was your problem before," she teased.

"Stop it." I knew I shouldn't have said the words before they left my mouth, but now there was no going back.

"I don't think I will. Anyway, you know he's a plumber."

I closed my eyes and drained my coffee quickly, ignoring the heat. "Of course he is."

"And of course you know, because I'm sure you two already talked about it. And I know that you need a plumber after that jackhole walked out on you."

She fluttered her eyelashes as she said it, and I sighed. "I do, but I'm sure he's busy."

"His family does some fantastic work up here, and his cousins own Montgomery Inc. down in Denver."

I frowned, confused. "His cousins own a tattoo shop? How does that have anything to do with his current job?"

She waved me off. "No, they own Montgomery Inc., I-N-C, the huge construction company that started off as a small family business and is now doing eco-friendly builds like they are up here with Montgomery Builders. Same family, two different branches, but quite friendly. They also own Montgomery Ink, I-N-K, the tattoo shop I know you've gotten a tattoo at before."

I looked down at my forearm, at the Irish knot hidden beneath the leaves I had inked a year ago.

"They did a fucking incredible job. Should have put two and two together, with the name Montgomery."

She waved me off. "Montgomery isn't too much of a

unique name, but they are related. However, though Montgomery Builders up here is busy, I'm sure they could fit you in since you are a neighbor."

"I'm Evelyn and Robert's neighbor." And they were moving. I wasn't sure I could handle any new family in that house. And if they had kids? I held back a shudder as the coffee settled awkwardly in my stomach.

"And *my* neighbor, and I still love you."

I rolled my eyes. "Thanks for being so helpful."

"I noticed you didn't say I love you too, but I understand. We're not quite there yet in our relationship."

She smiled coyly, and I had to wonder if I had hurt her by not saying it. I didn't know if I could. She seemed to understand my hesitance but didn't say anything about it. After all, she knew exactly why I lived here, and why I wouldn't say *I love you.*

"Anyway, you should ask the boy."

"Boy," I repeated. There was nothing *boy* about Archer Montgomery. He was all man. Not that I was allowing myself to think that.

"Younger than both of us. But still a man. And he has sad eyes."

I stiffened, wondering why she was bringing that up. "Sad eyes."

"Yes. Sad, sad eyes. Handsome ones, though."

That made me snort. "You should ask him out then."

"I didn't mention that you should, but he's not my type. He could be yours."

There was no way I was continuing this line of conversation. "You don't know my type, Penny. And I'm not interested in dating or whatever."

"Sometimes it's the *or whatever* that's the fun part. Talk with him. See if he can help. I'm sure there are a few things that you could help him with." She winked as she said it, and I narrowed my eyes.

"Penny."

"I meant construction things. Not sexual things. Unless you would like to do sexual things, and then that would be remarkable, wouldn't it? He is a piece."

"You're incorrigible."

"I try. Now, go talk with him. He looks like he could use a friend."

And there it was. "I'm not in the habit of making friends, Penny."

"No, you're not, Killian Hart. But you should be. Because I love you. And maybe you should try—just a little."

And with that, she walked away, taking my coffee cup and my dog with her.

I frowned when Cora followed her outside and shook my head. She would return Cora later, I knew it, but they hadn't even talked to me about it first. Well then.

I got my water bottle, filled it up, and started to get back to work. I had framing on the back half of the house to work on since it was a complete rebuild, and with the setbacks I'd had recently with the trash, broken instruments, and flaky workers, I was behind.

Not that I had a real deadline.

I didn't have to work for money, didn't have to work at all. I owned this piece of land outright and could just work on it until I died.

With that chilling thought, I did my best to shift my focus.

A couple of hours later, the sound of someone singing a soft melody echoed throughout the trees, and I moved slightly to see Archer walking around, taking notes, and moving stacks of bricks.

I frowned, wondering why I was paying attention all of a sudden. Evelyn and Robert had been around before, and I hadn't noticed them, not really, but apparently this guy just kept making me see him.

I wasn't in the mood.

Archer seemed to notice me watching him and turned, his eyes wide.

I could have turned away, pretended that I hadn't seen him, but that would require caring. Archer gave me a small smile, waved, and moved towards me.

I sighed, knowing that I should have just walked away.

Then Cora burst out of the bushes, barking happily, and Archer grinned, going to his knees a few feet in front of me as Cora lapped at his face.

"Well, hello. You're gorgeous."

I swallowed hard and cleared my throat. "Cora, let the man breathe."

"Cora is yours then? Beautiful dog, she doesn't even

seem to notice she is missing a leg, and so *sweet*." There was a pointed way he said it, and I had a feeling he was wondering why such a sweet dog would be with an asshole like me. I asked myself that daily.

"Cora. Back. Sit."

She listened, sat down on her haunches, her torso held up by only her front left leg, and let her tongue loll out, looking adorable as can be. I didn't even notice the missing leg anymore, and like Archer said, she really didn't seem to, either.

Archer wiped his face, grinning as he stood up. "I've always wanted a dog, but it's hard for me to bring them to my workplaces all the time."

"That would be difficult, and I would hate leaving them at home for hours a day." I hadn't even meant to say that out loud, or even speak at all, but here I was. I blamed Penny for this. It seemed the easiest.

"Yeah, that was my thinking. So, it's just you and Cora out here?" he asked, looking around.

"Yep. In our hermit serial-killer ways."

Again, with the humor. Who the fuck was I?

Archer's eyes widened for a minute before he grinned. His whole face lit up, and he just looked happy.

I cleared my throat. "Anyway. Yes, the two of us."

"It's a great place up here."

"Are you thinking of buying it?" I asked, curious even though I didn't want to be.

"It's pretty far away from my job and my family." Archer

sighed. "All of my siblings and their spouses and babies and my parents are all in the Fort Collins area. It doesn't make sense for me to move out here alone when I work with them, and I like being near them."

"Makes sense." However, I didn't know why I felt a little relieved about the fact that Archer didn't have anyone waiting for him at home.

What the hell was wrong with me?

"Anyway, I'm just getting back to work, my team is setting up tomorrow, and we're going to be doing a few demo things, and then I have to get at the plumbing."

That sparked a question, and I tried to hold it back, but Archer seemed to understand I wanted to say something. *How did I know that?*

"What is it?" he asked.

I shrugged. "My plumber dropped the ball and left the project without a word, taking my money with him."

Archer's eyes narrowed. "Who was it?"

"Thompson and Sons Plumbing."

Archer's eyes widened. "Really? Oh, I guess that makes sense now. It used to actually be Thompson and Sons, and then the cousins bought them out, and they haven't been the same. Shit, I'm sorry. I hope it wasn't too much money?"

I shook my head, my hands on my hips. "No. It was only the deposit. I'm still pissed off. And I'm not in the mood to deal with the Better Business Bureau."

"I hear you. Well, I can give you some references. Or recommendations."

"My neighbor keeps saying I should talk to you," I grumbled, wondering why the hell I wouldn't just shut up.

"Penny? She's a hoot." Archer grinned again, and I turned my gaze away from him.

"She's something. And yeah, recommendations would be helpful."

"If I can take a look at your house at one point, I can see who would work best, or hell, I can try to fit you into the schedule."

I looked at him then, wondering why he sounded so down and why I was even caring. "You don't have to do any of that. I'll find someone."

"Then I'll help you find the best. Well, *I'm* the best, and if I can't work on it, then I can find you the second best." He winked, though the humor didn't quite reach his eyes, and I just sighed.

"I need to get back to work. I'm rebuilding most of the house."

Archer's eyes widened, and I saw the interest in them, but I didn't offer for him to come see it. I didn't do anything. Because there was that pull there, that attraction, and I didn't want it.

I couldn't have it.

And, as I remembered my dream from that morning, felt the ice slide over me again, I straightened. Archer seemed to notice the new look wash over me as he swallowed hard. "Anyway, I'll let you get back to it. It was nice to meet you,

Cora." Archer leaned down, slid his hands over Cora's flank. "Have a good day. I'll see you around."

And with that, he walked away, his shoulders slightly down, and I held back a curse.

I really was that asshole, but I couldn't change.

And as I remembered the ice, I knew I didn't want to.

Chapter Five

Archer

"What do you mean you're not in the mood for cheese?" Leif asked, his eyes wide.

I quickly hushed him, turning around to make sure that nobody was paying attention to us. Of course, the entire room had quieted because they all heard.

"I ate homemade macaroni and cheese yesterday, and I thought I would try a veggie plate today instead of going full cheese. I'm sorry."

Annabelle came up to me and handed over my nephew. Jack reached up and patted my cheek before laying his head on my shoulder.

"If you don't want cheese, hold a baby. That'll help whatever the hell's going on in your mind."

"Don't say hell around our kid," Jacob muttered, holding the other twin, Hailey.

My lips quirked, and I just smiled at my family. "I was in the mood for comfort food yesterday and made that five-cheese layered baked macaroni and cheese of mine. I'll have leftovers for days, but I forgot about dinner tonight while I was making it. I craved it and was so focused on making that macaroni and cheese that I didn't stop to think that maybe my arteries and stomach can't handle that much cheese so many days in a row."

"Okay, that's a decent excuse," Leif said as he folded his arms over his chest. "I don't know, though. I may have to tell my dad."

I narrowed my eyes at my second-cousin. "Okay then. That's just playing dirty. You know your dad, even if he's nearly two decades older than me, can kick my ass."

"Stop saying A-S-S in front of the baby," Annabelle whispered as she put her hands over Jack's ears.

"I'm sure they've all heard worse in this family," Brenna teased as she checked her phone. Her baby, as well as Beckett and Eliza's kid, were sleeping in the nursery. Paige and Lee were just now going up to put theirs in the nursery as well.

My parents had taken one of the spare guestrooms, ones that any number of Montgomerys had used in the past, and made a full-scale nursery, with multiple cribs, changing tables, and anything a growing baby could need. It didn't matter that we all lived within easy driving distance. They wanted grandparent time and were having a blast with it.

I knew as the kids grew up to big-kid beds, they'd have those of their own too. It was nice the way that we all banded together and that everybody was growing in ways and finding each other.

I loved my nieces and nephews. They were fantastic individuals and brought so much joy to my life.

I might only be slightly jealous that I didn't have one of my own, but that didn't take away any of the happiness and life I felt for the new babies in the Montgomery family.

"Okay, I understand, no cheese plate." My mother moved forward and plucked my nephew from my arms.

"Let's put the kids down for their N-A-P, and then we will find some vegetables in this house for you." She rolled her eyes, even though I knew she was joking.

The Montgomerys might joke that we were part of a cheese cult and that cheese was life. And while all of that was probably true, well, mostly true, it wasn't the whole of it. We still ate healthily and introduced new foods to our palates without involving cheese. Scary, but it happened.

I looked over at Leif as the rest of my siblings milled around the house, helping my parents with one thing or another, or just catching up with their spouses. Since we all worked together, we spent a lot of time with one another. However, it was rare we were all together at the same time as often as we used to be, thanks to babies, new families, and just life.

Hell, I was spending a lot of my time in the mountains now. I could do most of my work that I would need to do in the office from my computer, and as long as I had internet, I didn't need much.

Okay, maybe I needed a little bit more.

Leif pressed his shoulder against mine as he stared at me. I blinked, surprised that he was a little taller than me. When did that happen?

Probably about the time the kid had finished puberty and was no longer a kid. It still surprised me daily that this kid was only a few years younger than me. Time didn't make much sense.

"What's wrong?" Leif asked, and I shook my head.

"Nothing's wrong. Maybe I just ate too much cheese."

"You keep saying these things, and your family's going to think that there's something wrong with you. At least that's what my family would think."

"True. I am glad that you're here for this, though. I thought you would head back down to Denver."

"I am, later tonight after dinner. I want to go see the twins and Colin."

"You have pictures?" I asked, grinning.

Leif smiled and pulled out his phone. The twins were around two now, with Colin around eight if I was doing my math right. There were too many babies in the Montgomerys, and I couldn't keep it straight.

In the photo, Leif had Colin on his back and held each

of the twins in his arms. They were all grinning, their bright eyes shining.

Although Colin was Austin and Sierra's only biological child, they all had that Montgomery glow. Maybe it was the cheese, or maybe it was just the way that we surrounded each other with family.

"I need to make it down there. I have another piece that I want to add to my back, and I think it's your aunt's turn, not your dad's."

Leif grinned. "Aunt Maya will kick your ass if you skip her. You know the rule in the Montgomery family. You take turns with your family tattoos."

I rubbed my forearm—where my Montgomery iris lay—and grinned. Each of the Montgomerys had our crest, a tattoo that we literally inked on our bodies once we found the right place and the time was right. Nobody said you had to do it, but we all wanted it. Some people's were small, some were intricately woven into huge pieces, so it was like finding Waldo with the crest. Mine was interwoven within the vines and trees on my forearm.

I knew that Leif was slowly working on his own tattoos but was taking his time. He was nearly a blank canvas, but he was also an artist. His father and Maya, as well as our cousin down in Colorado Springs, had each done a tattoo on him. But, so far, that was it. He was figuring out what he wanted and, considering Leif was only twenty, I didn't blame him for taking time.

We may like ink as much as our cheese, but we were careful with it because ink was forever.

Just like the Montgomerys were.

"Did you hear Lee's getting his?" Leif asked, and I blinked.

"Really? I didn't."

"Someone said my name?" my brother-in-law said as he came forward and squeezed Leif's shoulders before he did mine.

Lee was our friend, and had been long before he had married Paige. It had been a shock when he had not only fallen in love with my baby sister but was raising the child she'd had with her ex-boyfriend as his own. Colton had walked away, maybe with a second glance, but not a third, but Lee had stepped up, and now they were a happy family and he was my brother-in-law, rather than the guy who I had once almost hooked up with when we had both been too drunk and realized we were far better as friends.

Thank God for that, because there were some things that Montgomerys did not need to share.

"I was just saying that you're getting your tattoo," Leif put in.

Lee grinned. "Yep. It's going to go on my shoulder piece once your dad works out the crest that he wants. Got to get my Irish folklore in there as well to mix with the Montgomerys."

"I can't believe it. You're branded. Even though you didn't take our name."

Paige sidled up to her husband and wrapped her arm around his waist. Lee didn't even have to look down at her before he had his arm around her shoulders, and they sank in together as if they had been doing this forever.

They just fit. And it surprised me that I hadn't seen it before.

I should have, but I hadn't.

"There's nothing wrong with being a Grier. I like being Paige Grier."

"Paige Montgomery-Grier," our dad grumbled from the deck, where he stood past the open French doors.

Paige just rolled her eyes and leaned into her husband. "I'm hyphenated. Just like Annabelle. It's a little ridiculous, but it happens."

I shrugged because I hadn't hyphenated. I hadn't even taken Marc's name. In retrospect, that should've been a sign, but Marc hadn't wanted to be a Montgomery, and he hadn't cared if I changed my name or not.

I had felt hurt at first, wondering why he didn't want me to be hyphenated or why he didn't want to hyphenate either, but in the end, it had saved paperwork, so I guess there was that.

"Okay, dinner's ready. Your dad is just getting the brisket out now, and I have the tamales."

I rubbed my hands together and waved to the other guys to go help my mom finish setting the table.

"These look amazing, Mom, thanks." I kissed the top of her head as she smiled at me.

"Eliza and I had fun making them."

I looked over at my sister-in-law as she sat next to her husband, Beckett.

"It's a recipe that one of my brothers got from Texas."

"So, your six hot brothers are all down south, and I'm still here," Paige said with a sigh and a flutter of her eyelashes.

Lee scowled down at her. "You're damn right they're down south. They can stay in Texas. Your married ass is going to stay up here."

Paige laughed as Beckett and Benjamin both growled at Lee for daring to mock-yell at our sister. Annabelle just giggled and took a seat next to me as Brenna took a seat next to Eliza.

We had pinto beans, cornbread, tamales, pico de gallo, brisket, green beans with bacon, some cheese for a small cheese plate, and an entire crudité vegetable plate.

I groaned at the amount of food in front of us but, considering how many people were at the table now, we needed this much food.

Jacob and Annabelle grinned at each other as they spoke in hushed tones. Eliza and Beckett looked like they were ready to swoon over one another, even as Eliza picked up her phone to check on Lexington in the crib.

Benjamin and Brenna were laughing at something that my father said, while Paige and Lee were still mock-arguing about the Wilder brothers while my dad put in his opinion.

I just sighed and looked over at Leif, who shrugged.

Everybody had started to feed themselves, so I did the same, wondering how I ended up nearly the only single one at the table, other than Leif—who had never been in a serious relationship ever, and wasn't even old enough to drink.

I was one step away from the kiddie table, and I needed to stop feeling sorry for myself.

"These are amazing," Paige exclaimed as she bit into another tamale.

"I'm going to have to tell my brother you said that. It was a long, arduous process even to get him to give us the recipe," my sister-in-law said with a laugh.

Mom beamed. "It was so much fun making them. We used to have them every Christmas Eve when I was a kid."

"Really?" Leif asked, echoing my thoughts.

"Yes. My mom and her mom used to make them for us, and we sort of got out of the habit of making them. I don't know why. There were just so many other things to eat. But we fell in love with cheese, and we never looked back," Mom said with a sigh.

My mother was Leif's grandfather's sister. Though none of us had met our grandpa or grandma before they had passed, I knew that Austin, Leif's father, had.

We were all a big tangled mess of family and connections, but I liked hearing the stories of things we had missed in the past.

"Anyway, speaking of family traditions, I have news."

We all looked at her as we continued to eat, and I frowned at the odd look that Mom gave me.

"As you know, we try to do a family reunion every three years because there are so many new babies, and we just want to celebrate as often as we can."

"Oh, it's this year, isn't it?" Annabelle asked. "Are Aunt Marie and Uncle Henry doing it?"

"No, they aren't," Mom said with a grin.

My eyes widened.

"Mom?" I whispered.

"Marie and Henry have done it often because they have the most property, and since they have eight kids and had the first set of grandkids, it made sense. And then it went down to Katherine and William in Colorado Springs, and then Timothy and Francine over in Boulder. We've all rotated who host it, even as we went from every five years to three years, to sometimes one or two years between the reunions because we just want to spend time together. This time, though, it's going to be here. In Fort Collins, at this house. Because we have the space, and it's time for us to join in the Montgomery festivities."

My dad smiled at his wife as tears slowly slid down my mom's cheeks.

Everybody started talking at once, and I leaned over and hugged my mom tightly.

"That's amazing news, Mom."

"Couldn't have done it without you kids. I love you."

She kissed my cheek and leaned against my shoulder as

everyone continued to talk about the upcoming reunion and the fact that we were going to have more Montgomerys than ever.

My mother and father had been in a semi-feud with the other Montgomerys for as long as I could remember. And it was all because my father had somehow felt inadequate or that he wasn't part of the other Montgomerys. His name had been Montgomery, and we had a whole other set of Montgomery relatives that had nothing to do with the Colorado Montgomerys. When he had moved here, he had found my mother, Pamela Montgomery, and they had fallen in love and gotten married. That meant she hadn't even had to change her name when they wed and were in no way related at all. Not even eighth cousins, from what we could tell. And then my dad had gotten in a fight with my mother's three brothers, and though they had tried to be cordial for the kids, it had been a glaring issue when it came to the fact that we had similar businesses, and we were a big family.

Things were mended now, and they spent a lot of time together. The eight of them had even gone on a cruise together.

The fact that we were having the reunion here was astounding. Not because Uncle Harry and Aunt Marie tried to force hosting the reunion at their house all the time. It had always just made sense to be there because they had the space. They had the means.

But now all of us did, and this was going to be a lot of

work, but with the way that my mom smiled, I would do anything for her.

"Archer, darling, while I have your attention, can I ask you for something?" Mom asked, after a moment, and I turned to her, smiling.

"Of course. What is it?"

"I know you're busy with your other project and work, but I could use some help. Will you be my right arm for this reunion? Your father will help, of course, but he's not the best at planning events like this. He'll be there to do whatever I need him to do, but I need a planner."

I froze. "Wouldn't Paige be a better planner? She's amazing at it. Not that I won't, Mom. I will. But why didn't you ask Paige? Or Annabelle, or anybody else other than me who is good at planning? I am good at parties, but this is a huge-scale thing and a lot of responsibility."

"I would, Archer, but with the new baby, I don't want to take her time away from Lee and Emery. You understand, don't you?"

I smiled, ignoring the weird twinge in my heart.

Nothing about what my mom had just said was wrong. It wasn't cruel, rude, and it shouldn't be painful.

Because it was true, everybody else had new babies at home and were exhausted a lot of the time because they were trying to do everything.

I was the only one without that, so it made sense that she would come to me for help, and yet why did it feel like I was once again being left behind?

"I'd love to help," I lied as I smiled hard.

No one else seemed to have heard what we were talking about as we continued to speak, and I just shook my head and continued eating, knowing I needed to get over it.

By the time we cleaned up, and I promised my mom we would speak soon about the reunion, I was exhausted. I said goodbye to the others and headed home.

I walked into my empty apartment, slid my shoes off, put my keys and phone on the front table, and picked up the mail that I had discarded earlier.

I thumbed through it, wondering if I should have a beer or maybe just an aspirin and go to bed early.

I had a lot of work to do, and I wanted to spend the afternoon out on the mountain.

That would help. Maybe.

The thick envelope surprised me, and I frowned at the embossed signature and beauty of it.

A wedding invitation.

To me? Who did I know who was getting married?

There was no return address, so I opened the actual wax seal and pulled out the invitation.

The envelope, RSVP card, and everything else poured out of it as I stood there, transfixed. The words blended on the page for a minute, and I swallowed hard.

Marc Hastings and Rebecca Harrington cordially invite you to their wedding.

There were more words, things I should probably care about, but I just stared, not quite comprehending what I was seeing.

My ex-husband was marrying Rebecca Harrington.

I knew that name.

She was a partner at a law firm. Brilliant, icy, blonde, nearly Marc's height.

She was a powerhouse.

And perfect for Marc.

I hadn't even realized he was dating.

I looked down at the envelope, around my cold and empty apartment.

My ex-husband was getting married.

And, apparently, I was invited to the damn wedding.

Chapter Six

Killian

Cora bounced along to pass in front of me, and I shook my head, knowing that she was just anxious since I hadn't slept the night before.

I was so tired of nightmares. They just didn't seem to have any point, but it wasn't like I could stop them.

My phone buzzed again and I looked down at the read-out, knowing if I didn't answer now, my sister was never going to give up. In fact, she would probably fly up from Texas right now just to check on me.

And I didn't want to have her see me face-to-face.

I answered the phone and scowled at her face on my

screen. I hadn't realized it was a video call, and there was no going back now.

"You look wonderful. I love the little scowl for me. It makes me feel at home."

She fluttered her eyelashes, and I held back a growl.

"Hi, Ann."

"Hello, big brother. I love you."

"Is there a reason that you're calling?" I asked, and she sighed.

"I just wanted to check on you because you're my big brother. And I kind of like you."

"That makes one of us," I growled.

"Good to know you're still your usual self."

"Well, you must like my usual self since you keep calling."

"You're my brother. Of course, I'm going to call you."

"What is it, Ann? Everything okay down in the hellhole of Texas?"

"Stop calling it a hellhole. I like my little area."

"I'm just saying. They have hill country there that looks like the hill in my backyard rather than an actual range."

"Not everybody can be blessed with living in the Rocky Mountains. The elevation's too high for me anyway. You know my lungs don't like it."

I nodded, feeling a bit annoyed with myself for forgetting. Ann had terrible asthma, and while the high elevation and thin air might work for some people, it didn't for my sister. It was another reason why she didn't visit often and why I didn't want her to come. I didn't want my little sister to get hurt. Not because she was checking on my grumpy ass.

"Well, how is the hill country? Enjoying the mountainous peaks?"

She flipped me off, but I couldn't help but smile.

"Things are going okay here. I'm just working."

"I hope not too hard."

"I probably work less than you do, and you don't even need to work."

"I think building this house is work enough."

Other things were left unsaid. Like why I didn't need to work anymore, and why the settlement that I hadn't even asked for had made it so I would never have to lift a finger another day for the rest of my life.

No amount of money would change things, would make things better or make the money worth it. I would give it all up to have my old life back, but that wasn't happening any time soon.

"Anyway, I have news and wanted to be the one to tell you."

I froze at the cautious look on her face and as her teeth worried her lip.

"What's wrong? Are you sick? Fuck. I can fly down there. You know I don't want to go down there, but I will."

Her eyes brightened for a moment, even as they filled with tears.

"Shit. What's wrong, Ann?"

"Nothing's wrong. Not really."

"What the fuck do you mean by not really?"

"The fact that you would come down here, Killian, means the world to me. I love you so much."

"Talk to me."

"I'm pregnant, Killian."

I froze as memories assailed me, and I tried not to panic. Tried not to throw up.

"Ann. Congratulations." I smiled softly, even as my world broke apart and everything ached.

"I almost flew up there just to tell you in person."

"I'm going to be an uncle again. It's pretty amazing, baby sis."

"I just kind of...I love you, Killian. You're my favorite big brother."

"And you're my favorite little sister." I echoed the familiar refrain.

We talked for a few minutes more before Ann hung up and went back to work.

I just stared at my blank phone, wondering why I hated myself so much. Because my sister had been afraid to tell me she was pregnant with her third child. She hadn't wanted to hurt my feelings over something that should be joyous, momentous. Something that was going to bring her hope and happiness.

And I was the asshole that was holding her back.

I needed to stop. I needed to be better.

Yet, the nightmares wouldn't go away.

I slid my phone into my pocket and went down the path a little bit further, Cora leading me, and it wasn't until I was upon them that I realized where my meddling dog had led us.

Penny stood near my neighbor's house, Archer next to her, as the two laughed over something.

I frowned, wondering when the two had gotten so close and why any jealousy would even come at me.

It wasn't like Penny was my friend. Or at least my only friend. I didn't need to be her only friend.

Why did I feel weird?

At the sound of Cora's bark, she smiled wide and bent down to brush Cora's flank. My dog, the traitorous puppy, left Penny and went straight to Archer. She went on her hind legs and patted her paw against Archer's chest, and I scowled.

"Down, Cora. No jumping."

Cora gave me a look, and I could have sworn she rolled her eyes before she went down to all fours, and Archer knelt in front of her. He petted her, rubbing his hands up and down her body as he asked her if she was a good girl.

I rolled my eyes as Penny narrowed hers.

"Well, Hook. It seems that Cora brought us a nice surprise."

"Hook?" Archer asked as he raised a single brow.

Why did I like that look? Because he could arch it so perfectly, as if he had practiced in the mirror a thousand times?

He probably had.

"I like to call him Hook sometimes. He's like a blond Captain Hook to me. You know, the one from the show?"

"You even have the same name now that I think about it," Archer said, that smile on his face a little devilish.

"I was named far before the show ever came out. And Captain Hook isn't blond."

"He could be. You never know."

"Now I'm picturing that particular Captain Hook and that actor blond. It could work."

Archer and Penny shared a look and she sighed.

"Do you know, Archer? You remind me so much of my son sometimes."

I nearly tripped over my feet as I went to Penny, surprised she'd even said anything.

Penny never mentioned her son, just like I never mentioned my past. It was what we did. We circled around it, never actually having to say it out loud until things were better.

Or they weren't better at all, and I was just pretending. But I was good at just pretending.

"Oh really? What's his name?"

Penny smiled softly, and I wanted to punch Archer for daring to even bring this up, even though Penny was the one to say something in the first place.

"His name was Reggie. My Reggie. He was very handsome, like you. All dark looks but with light eyes. He smiled often, like you do, but he had a little secret spice underneath that always surprised people."

Archer's eyes went sad as he reached forward and gripped her hand softly.

"I'm sorry. I didn't mean to make you sad."

"It's okay. I lost my son the same way I lost my husband. In war. Reggie wanted to follow in his father's footsteps. And so much like when my husband passed, I had to stand on my doorstep as a military chaplain and another serviceman stood there to tell me that they were gone. It never gets any easier, no matter how you learn to deal with it."

Archer was up in a second, moving faster than I could. He wrapped his arms around her. He hugged her tight and, to no one's surprise, Penny hugged right back.

"You're a good boy, Archer Montgomery."

"I'm sorry that I remind you of him. That's got to be difficult."

"No, no. I like to be reminded. Hiding away my pain day-in and day-out does me no good. It's good to let it out."

She didn't have to look at me for me to know that she was talking directly to me.

"Anyway, I need to go back and work on my loom."

"What are you working on?" Archer asked, and he seemed interested.

"Just a commission piece. I sell my wares at local festivals and in any shop that will take me. It's nice to keep my hands busy, even as the arthritis hits."

I leaned forward, past Archer, and kissed Penny on the top of the head. "Let me know if you need me to move anything around. I know you've got that huge shipment coming in, you don't have to do that alone."

"What would I do without my handsome and strong and virile neighbor?"

She winked as she said it, patted Cora on the head, then waved goodbye, leaving me standing there.

"Virile?" Archer asked, that brow raised again.

"She's lost her mind. It's okay, though. She's sweet."

"Whatever you say, Hook."

"Just call me Killian. I'm not a fan of Captain Hook."

"Because of the gators? Or because he keeps chasing around a boy that will never grow up that wears green tights?"

"Maybe just because she wanted to put me in eyeliner one day," I mumbled, and Archer threw his head back and laughed, bringing a smile to my face.

"I didn't know you would be up here so quickly," I said as I looked around.

"My team was up here yesterday, and they'll be up tomorrow. I just needed to get out."

"Oh," I said to him, while wondering if I should say anything more.

"If it's too loud for you, I'm sorry. Renovations do that."

I shrugged. "I'm over here doing the same thing, but I don't have a full team."

"Are you going to let me look around and let you know

for the plumbing thing?" Archer asked as he put his hands in his pockets. I stared at him, at those blue eyes of his, and wondered why he looked so off. I didn't even know him, but I felt like something was wrong with him.

He looked like he was unsure of himself, and from what I knew about this guy, from the first moment he fell on me from a roof, he wasn't the type of guy to be like this.

Or maybe I was just losing my mind.

"You can come to take a look," I said, surprising myself.

From the look on Archer's face, he was equally surprised. "Okay, sure. Let's go do it."

"Now?"

"I don't have anything better to do."

"Really? Should it worry me that you don't have enough work to do? If you have the time to look at my place, then that means you have too much spare time, right?"

"I'm supposed to take today off, and instead of doing paperwork or paying bills or watching the game, I decided to come up here and just think."

I frowned at him before I started walking, Cora at my side. He followed just behind us.

We made it around the bend to my place, and Archer let out a whistle.

"This place is going to be amazing."

"What, it's not amazing now with half of it unfinished?" I asked dryly.

"Are you trying to get growly with me, or are you just enjoying yourself?"

"Whatever you need to believe."

"Okay then," Archer whispered.

"What's wrong then? Why do you need to be here to think?"

I could have rightly kicked myself. Why did I care? Fuck. I was here because I didn't want to think at all, and yet all I could do was think, to dream, and now I was asking someone else what they were worried about. It wasn't my business, and I didn't fucking care. Only, I did seem to care, and it worried me.

"My ex-husband is getting married."

I blinked and looked up at him. "I didn't know you used to be married."

"I wasn't married that long. We didn't work out."

"Was he an asshole?" I asked, growling a bit even though I didn't know why.

Archer's lips twitched before his face fell. "Maybe. I don't know. And that was the problem. I didn't know. I should have, but I just didn't see how we weren't a good fit until it was too late, and then we just broke up. I walked away because I wasn't the man that he needed me to be, and I didn't know if I had married the man that I thought he was, or the man he actually was."

"So, he wasn't an asshole then, not really?"

"Maybe a little. I don't know. Anyway, he's getting married. To a woman named Rebecca."

"I see." I frowned. "No, I don't see. Does that surprise you?"

Archer blinked and looked up at me. "That he's marrying a woman? No. I knew his sexuality before, and hell, I've dated women before too."

"Makes sense."

"Yeah. That's not the problem. And honestly, I know a little bit about this woman, and she totally fucking fits him like a glove."

"So, what's the problem?" I asked.

Archer just sighed. "Because my ex-husband's getting married, and I don't know what to think about it. There shouldn't be a problem, but there is because I'm making it one." He just sighed. "I don't really want to talk about it anymore."

I nodded. "Okay. Fine. Forget I asked."

"But thank you for asking. I haven't told my family that he's getting married yet, and it feels weird to me that I hadn't."

"Are you close to your family?"

Archer laughed, and I had to wonder if I had said something wrong.

"What?" I asked.

"Sorry. I forget that not everybody knows my family. Yes. We're close. Really close."

"I met your cousin. Austin? He did my tattoo."

Archer grinned. "Small world. If you want a good tattoo, you go to my family."

"And you guys are close. Why didn't you tell them?"

"No reason yet. I will."

"Did they like the guy?"

"No. Which should have been the first clue. They tolerated him and did their best to love him. But it never worked out. It never felt right. Again, I didn't see it until it was too late. Either way, it's fine. I'm fine."

I didn't know if I actually believed his words, but I didn't question him. It wasn't my place to say, and honestly, I was already asking way too much as it was. I wasn't usually this talkative, and I shouldn't care this much.

"Why don't I show you the place?" I asked after a moment, clearing my throat.

"Okay. Sounds good to me. What are you thinking for it?"

"I have plans, sketches, and maps with everything from the old company."

Archer nodded. "Well, show me. And I will tell you what you need."

I looked up at him then, swallowed hard, and wondered why those words bothered me.

Because I didn't need anything. Not anything Archer could give me.

And as that cold realization slid over me, I knew that I needed to get him out of this house quickly.

Because there was nothing for me here.

There hadn't been before, and even with Archer here, nothing changed.

It never would.

Chapter Seven

Archer

"I can hate him if you want," Brenna said as she put her head on my shoulder.

The music was blasting. People were laughing, drinking, eating good food, and just enjoying themselves. That's what happened when you went to Riggs'. Our friend knew how to cater to his clientele and made this bar perfect. You felt safe here, and you could have fun here. Or at least you could if you weren't slowly falling into a fit of depression because your ex-husband was getting married seemingly out of nowhere.

I looked around the bar at the gleaming black wooden and metallic surfaces and tried to put on a smile. We had rebuilt a lot of this after it had been damaged by vandalism over a year ago.

Riggs had to deal with his ex-husband and a past he hadn't wanted to reclaim. I hadn't blamed him at all, and now he and Clay were happily married, raising those three kids, and enjoying themselves—even though I didn't know how they had time to breathe, let alone have a happy marriage. And they *looked* happy.

And here I was, feeling like I was losing my mind because I was jealous over a woman I didn't know, and not because she was marrying my ex-husband. No, because somehow, I wasn't good enough.

I had never been good enough for Marc, and he had made it clear to me, even though I had tried.

I just didn't know how I could fix it.

"Seriously. I know people are day-drinking right now since it's the middle of an afternoon for an event at this bar, but you can pay attention to me."

I looked down at my friend and sister-in-law and sighed. "I'm sorry, Brenna. What were you saying?"

She crossed her eyes and blew out a breath. "That I can beat up your ex? If you want. I promise I'll be gentle. Or not."

I snorted and then took a sip of my club soda. I wasn't in the mood to drink today, mostly because if I did, I wouldn't stop, because I just wanted to forget about the annoyance of that stupid wedding invitation. And how I reacted around Killian. I was such a bumbling idiot when it came to him.

Why? Well, probably because the first time I had met him, I had literally thrown myself on top of him by falling off a roof. That was not the greatest meet-cute, not that there needed to be a meet-cute because there wasn't anything cute about it. Yes, he was cute, but I didn't want him. I didn't want to date at all, and I just needed to get the fuck over myself.

And why was I even thinking about Killian when I was supposed to be thinking about fucking Marc?

"I don't need you to beat up my ex-husband. We don't even need to think about him."

"He sent you a wedding invitation. Why the hell would he do that?"

"Are we discussing the fact that you got a wedding invitation from Marc?" Benjamin asked as he slid his arm around his wife's shoulders.

They leaned into each other without even thinking, and once again I ignored the slight pain in my heart.

They were just so perfect for each other even though they had spent years just being friends. I hadn't even realized there had been an attraction between them, and frankly, I didn't think they had either. If anything, I had thought Brenna had once had a thing for Beckett. Instead, it had been for his twin. I was not firing on all cylinders when it came to romance and finding your one true love. Everyone else seemed to be doing it, but I was behind. Again.

"I didn't even realize he was dating again," Benjamin said as he slid his hand over his beard. He was letting it grow out longer than he had in the past, and now you could tell the difference between him and Beckett. Not that I had ever struggled to tell them apart. I always knew which brother was which.

Benjamin used to be the quieter one, the one deeper in his thoughts, but Brenna had opened him up, so now I saw the happiness and peacefulness in his gaze. While Beckett had been the growlier one, the one who thought he had the weight of the world on his shoulders, since he was the eldest. It was only by a few minutes, but Beckett took that role of oldest brother seriously.

Now, thanks to Eliza, he laughed more.

Annabelle smiled more, took more time for herself, and believed in herself more because of Jacob. And Paige, well, Paige brought new life to who she was and bubbled just as effusively as ever because of Lee.

Each of them was already amazing, profoundly talented, and layered, and falling in love with the right person had only shined a light on who they could be, instead of changing them into something that they weren't.

"You guys, this is a party, an event where we're supposed to enjoy ourselves, have a beer, and not think about the fact that I got a little envelope that I'm not going to worry about."

"You're not going to the wedding, are you?" Annabelle asked as she stomped towards me.

My twin and I didn't have the twin intuition that others did. I wasn't even sure Beckett or Benjamin did. But no matter what happened, I knew I could always go to her. When I had left Marc, and I had nowhere else to go, I had gone to her. Yes, I could have gone to any one of my siblings, even my parents. Hell, my cousins would have taken me in, in an instant. Some of them even had multiple homes I could have gone to and just stayed and hidden.

I hadn't done any of that. I had gone to Annabelle. Because she was my twin, part of my heart, and held a sliver of my soul. She had taken it from me when we were born, just like I held hers.

And when she went through her own hell before, I had been at her side. I wouldn't push her away or get angry about the fact that I wasn't doing the greatest job at the moment remaining sane or acting as if I wasn't wallowing in my own sadness. I hated that about me, and I didn't want that to be part of my life. I didn't like being this person, so I needed to stop and get over myself. Only, it was easier to think than to actually do it.

"I'm not going to the wedding. I will RSVP no, though, because I'm not a rude asshole."

"You do not have to even RSVP," Brenna grumbled.

"You make wedding cakes. You're a brilliant and talented award-winning cake decorator. You deal with weddings. You should know that you just can't *not* RSVP to something," I muttered.

"You so can. You haven't spoken to him at all since the divorce, right?" At my nod, Brenna continued. "And he just sends you an invitation out of the blue? It's not being nice.

He's not trying to mend fences or be friends. If he would've done that, he would've given you a warning or would've said, 'Hey, I'm dating. Meet my girlfriend.' No, he sends the invite to rub your face in it because he's an asshole, just like he always was." She looked down at her empty drink and handed the glass to Benjamin. "And I have clearly had too many drinks. I can't believe I just said that." Tears started to fall down her cheeks, and I cursed under my breath before I pulled her out of Benjamin's arms and hugged her tight.

"No, you're right. You said everything right."

"I'm not the one that usually says these things. That's Annabelle. Or Paige."

"I only heard the last of that, but that does sound like something I would say. I'm so proud of you, Brenna. Because you said what we were all thinking," Paige exclaimed.

I narrowed my eyes at all of them as I pulled away from Brenna and wiped her tears away. She immediately sank into her husband's side and he soothed her.

Everybody was paired up and happy, all eight of them surrounding me.

And I just wanted to scream.

How was I a ninth wheel? I hadn't even realized that was a thing until here I was, a ninth wheel. Of course, Paige had once said she was one before, but now I know that wasn't true. I was the one destined to be alone.

And maybe I needed a drink if I was going to utter those words in my head, like a selfish little idiot.

"Okay, I won't RSVP. I will burn the letter instead of letting it sit on my front table mocking me whenever I walk in the door."

"You haven't already shredded it?" Lee asked, his hand on Paige's shoulder.

"No. Didn't know what to do. So I've been ignoring it."

"If it's at your front door, you can't."

"If I keep putting other pieces of paper on it, I can. It will just lie under a stack of bills until I notice it a year later."

"Because you can totally let all that mess just pile up," Eliza teased.

I pinched the bridge of my nose. "Could we talk about something else? Anything else? Has a baby done something new? Why don't I have any new pictures of my nieces or nephews?"

Immediately, they each pulled all their phones and showed me the pictures of the next generation doing extraordinary things. Like smiling, coloring, walking. All these babies could do so many things, and while my paternal clock was slightly ticking, I ignored it because I could do this. I would be the best gay uncle there was—the guncle of life.

I didn't need Marc or wedding invitations or pity. I had this. I didn't need anything else.

"I am stealing this handsome guy right now from whatever's going on even though I love seeing the pictures of the kids because I need help behind the bar."

I peered at Riggs as he pulled his dark hair back from his face, his eyes dancing with laughter.

"Why? Because I'm the sober one?" I teased.

"Yes, and I could use your help."

"Because everybody else has something to do," I muttered.

"No, because I'm saving you. Goodbye now, goodbye," Riggs teased as he pulled me past Clay and the others and behind the bar.

Riggs, of course, left a huge smacking kiss on Clay's lips as everybody cheered, and others began to enjoy their party.

"I can't believe you're working for Clay's party."

"This is just an excuse for everyone to drink in the middle of the afternoon and enjoy themselves. I don't mind, it's paying the bills, and Clay did land that huge account, did amazing on it, and Beckett is so proud that we're having the party here. I am a proud husband."

"And you need me to help with drinks? Or maybe be the bar back?"

"I'm shocked you didn't say anything sexual about that," Riggs said as he leaned against the bar. "I mean, usually you're outstanding with the *that's what she said* joke."

I sighed. "I must be losing my touch."

"Again, no joke."

"I promise I'll make a dick joke later."

"That's all I ask. We do need those dick jokes."

I snorted and held up my hands. "Okay. What do you need?

"Again, I'm trying to be good." Riggs' eyes twinkled, and I couldn't help but laugh.

"You better because your husband is bigger than me and can hurt me. And he's staring this way."

Riggs looked over and winked and then pushed at my shoulder. "Okay. You just need to stand back here and look busy for a minute or two. I just wanted to get you away for a while because I know your family has the best intentions and care about you, but they also can be a lot. It's okay for you not to want to talk about your ex-husband."

The word had spread. "So I'm not an idiot for wanting to RSVP no?"

"I think you should. Either a huge red X in Sharpie, or a pointed 'No' with a 'Thank you so much for the invite, I wish you well. Bless your heart.'"

I laughed then and did indeed help him wash some of the glasses as we helped fill the servers' orders.

"I'm not Southern. I don't think 'bless your heart' works for me."

"I think you can handle it, unless you want to go. Bring a date. Make it a whole thing. And then you can fall madly in love with your date, and after a slight miscommunication, enjoy a happily ever after."

"How many Hallmark movies have you been watching?"

Riggs snorted. "None. But I have been listening to fantastic romances on audiobook while I've been working."

"Which ones?"

"The ones you recommended me. I'm going through your TBR now."

I sighed and continued washing the glasses. "I was hoping for new books to add."

"If I find them, I'll send them your way. I'm delighted that you signed me up for the library, though, because with Clay doing so well with you guys work-wise, we still have three kids to put through college and I don't think I can afford an audiobook habit."

I laughed as I worked with him. Even though he didn't need me, it was nice to keep my hands and my mind busy.

"I hear you're in charge of the reunion," Clay said as he sidled up to the bar. He had a list of orders in his hand, and Riggs slipped the notes from him.

"First, before you answer that, Clay, babe, why are you working?" Riggs asked.

Clay leaned forward and kissed his husband soundly on the mouth. I tried not to feel jealous. "I was bored without you. Sue me."

"It's a party for you. You're not supposed to be bored," Riggs ordered.

"And my husband shouldn't be working, but here we are. I'm not actually bored. I just wanted to see you."

"Please stop. The mush, it's killing me," I joked, not entirely teasing.

Both of the guys just rolled their eyes at me, kissed above the bar, and then turned to me.

"Reunion?" Clay asked.

"Yes, I'm helping Mom with the reunion."

"It's a big thing for Pamela to have it here."

Since Clay worked for us and had been in enough of our family squabbles, he knew precisely why it was a big deal. Clay had been introduced to us through our Denver Montgomery branch since he was practically godson to one of my cousins. Clay had been an honorary Montgomery for longer than I had known.

"It is a big deal, and all of the older generations of Montgomerys are putting in their two cents helping, but not being overbearing. Like they want Mom to shine."

I smiled as I said it, and Clay grinned. "That's good. So she's not overwhelmed?"

"Not yet, but we're still in the planning stages. And it's my job to help."

"Let me guess, because you have more free time?" Riggs asked wryly.

I cringed. "Got it in one."

"That's got to hurt." Clay winced.

"It shouldn't. It's my own thinking, and I'm over it."

"Well, that's a lie," Clay added.

"Okay, it's a lie. But I will get over it. And it's the truth, though, because everybody else *is* busy. We all are. The fact that we're doing this on a Wednesday afternoon when we all have work early tomorrow tells you just how busy we are."

"Which is great for Montgomery Builders and Riggs'," Clay added as he looked at his husband. "However, it does make a social life kind of difficult."

"When and if I ever date again, I don't know how I'd fit it in."

"Again, no joking?" Riggs asked, his hands in the air.

I just shook my head. "I'll get right back on top, I promise."

"You're killing me here," Riggs growled, before he went to the other side of the bar to help one of his staff. "Seriously, if you need anything, let me know. I don't know if it would be weird for you to ask your siblings for help even though you know they would do it in a heartbeat."

"I know. I just don't want them to think that I can't handle it. Or that I'm jealous."

Clay leaned forward. "Or maybe you could just tell them your true feelings, just like you made them do every single time that they were confused or conflicted."

"I don't like the fact that you are throwing my own actions and words in my face." I smiled when I said it, but it was kind of the truth.

"Get over it. It's what you made me do. Now, Annabelle might have mentioned that there might have been a hot guy that you fell on top of?" Clay hedged.

Riggs popped out from behind him quickly.

"What? Hot guy? You were on top of who? Why do we not have any details?"

I pushed Riggs at Clay, just laughed, and shook my head.

"So, what's his name? What does he look like? How did he feel pressed up against you? Okay, so tell me anything," Clay said as I just rolled my eyes.

"His name is Killian."

"Oh, that's a good name," they both said at the same time before they looked at each other, laughed, and promptly kissed.

I sighed, ignoring the jealous feeling again. I needed to get over myself.

Clay waved me on. "Killian. Well? What else?"

"He looks like Chris Hemsworth with a shorter haircut."

"What? You never said that!" Paige exclaimed as she practically jumped on the bar stool. "What else?"

"I didn't realize you were listening." I looked around and sighed at the women of my family as they moved forward.

"You said Chris Hemsworth. It was like a beacon," Annabelle declared as she came up to the bar, Eliza and Brenna right on her heels.

Thankfully, the guys were all still at the table, so I sighed.

"Well, he does. Like in Thor three, when they shaved the side of his head. He looks like that but with a bigger beard."

"Like the Chris Evans beard in Infinity War?" Paige asked, her hands clasped in front of her as she swooned.

"You're going to make Lee grow that beard, aren't you?" Brenna asked, teasing.

"I would say that you're already making Benjamin grow it, but he's my brother, and there are lines I just won't cross."

"What else?" Annabelle asked, and I scowled at Riggs and Clay, who were doing their best not to laugh and failing miserably.

"He's kind of an asshole."

"What kind of an asshole?" Paige asked as the laughter stopped.

"Not a Marc asshole. He doesn't put me down or anything."

They all stared at me, and I shrugged. "I wasn't unaware of what Marc did. I just knew he didn't mean to do it."

"Archer," Annabelle whispered, and I put my hand up.

"No, this is not about Marc. Or his wedding, or me being a fucking idiot for marrying him in the first place. You wanted to know all about Killian. Well, here it is. He's hot, blond, an asshole, a little broody, apparently good with his hands, and I honestly don't know what he felt like when I fell on him because I was falling from a fucking roof, and so all I could think about was my life flashing before my eyes, and not about the hot guy I landed on. Not until I scrambled off of him, feeling like an idiot."

They all stared at me then, and Paige raised her hand.

"What, Paige?" I asked, exasperated.

"Will you be seeing him again?"

They all grinned at me, and I threw my hands in the air.

"Probably, when I'm up there working. And if I do the plumbing at his house."

"Another joke missed," Riggs growled.

I just snorted. "Yes, another joke. Me working with his plumbing. Oh my God, I've never made that joke before, ever, in my long life as a plumber."

"You're just losing your touch, man." Riggs just shook his head, his expression forlorn.

"I'm going to see him again because I'm going to be working at the property next to him, but who knows if I'll ever talk to him. Maybe I'll talk to Cora, though."

"He has a wife?" Paige asked, her body deflating.

"She's beautiful, blonde, and perky."

"Are you talking about a dog or a very hot wife?" Annabelle asked, narrowing her eyes.

"You and that twin thing. Yes, she's a golden Lab, and amazing. She has three legs, can run faster than any dog I've ever seen, and I just want to cuddle her up and keep her away from the asshole man. But then I realize that he might be grumpy for a reason, and she keeps him sane. So I would never take Cora away from him."

"Aw, Killian and Archer kissing in a tree," Paige began singing.

"K-I-S-S-I-N-G," Eliza added.

I pointed at both of them. "I expected this from Paige, but you, Eliza? I thought better of you."

She just pointed at herself and arched a brow. "The youngest, with six brothers. I can take you, Archer. Any day, any time."

Everyone began talking at once, teasing me, but this time it felt okay. Maybe it was about a man that I would never actually speak to in a way that they wanted, but that was fine.

This was much better than before.

And I might see Killian again, but it wouldn't be for anything in a tree.

No, I was going to keep my feet firmly planted on the ground when it came to him.

No matter what.

Chapter Eight

Killian

I frowned at the cracks in the three windows in front of me before sipping my beer, trying not to get pissed off. It was odd since I didn't feel much of anything in the past couple of years.

I didn't feel joy in the slightest, as that feeling would never return. I didn't feel jealousy or anger. I couldn't feel anger. That would require me to be something more than I was.

But right then, anger slammed into me full force, and all I wanted to do was throw my beer bottle at the now broken windows and scream until the gods decided that they were going to be lenient on me.

"It doesn't make any fucking sense."

I had just put in these windows a month ago, and they were hurricane strength, triple-paned, the best you could buy for this area, so anyone who was inside during a fucking blizzard or windstorm would be fine in the mountains.

And yet, somehow, they had cracks all along the edges? It was as if somebody had taken a diamond or etching tool of some sort and carefully slid it across the corners of each of the panes. That, along with the stress from the wooden frames, and now cracks were starting to appear.

If the light hadn't hit it at just the right moment, I would've missed it this morning because they were so hairline. Yet, this looked almost deliberate.

I turned around, looked at the mountain behind me, the hills surrounding me, the massive trees, and figured it could be a stone, a rock, or fuck, a bird could have hit them. But all three large windows at once? No, that didn't make much sense. Especially not with the angle that these windows sat at since the whole reason I had put these windows in the great room was for the view. We were right on the edge of a hill so you could see for miles across the southern property line, with the mountains taking up space in the west, while the rest of the foothills were to the east.

I loved those windows.

Danielle had picked out those windows.

I swallowed hard, annoyed with myself for even thinking her name. I was so good about not thinking her name most of the time.

Cora whined beside me and I leaned down, brushed along her head, and took another sip of my beer.

"It's going to take months to order new windows."

"What happened?" Archer Montgomery asked as he walked down the path, his hands in his pockets, confusion on his face.

I hadn't heard him come up and I nearly jumped, but Cora's wagging tail had warned me he was there, so I hadn't thrown my beer bottle at him.

"I'm not sure. But all three are fucking broken now. I'm going to have to get them replaced."

Archer whistled out through his teeth. "It's a shame. Those are gorgeous."

"Yeah. They were custom for this design, and I don't know what the fuck I'm going to do now."

"Yeah, that's a hit to the budget."

I didn't tell him that I didn't care about the budget. I didn't need to worry about a budget anymore. Hell, I would do anything to worry about a fucking budget.

"Is your guy going to fix it?"

I turned to him then, looking him over. He wore dark jeans—not the jeans he worked in, but the jeans he went out in—a gray Henley with the sleeves rolled up to his shoulders, and his hair was a mess as if he'd been running his hands through it. He had on black boots, again, not work boots, so I didn't think he had come here to work.

Odd then, since he didn't own the fucking place, and

since he was walking around the forest in clothes that didn't fit the setting.

But what was I supposed to say to him? It wasn't like I should care. And the fact that I did just angered me more, on top of the broken windows.

"The guy that fit these in retired, so I'm going to have to find a new company."

Archer frowned. "What about for the rest of the house? Don't you have a company for those?"

"I do," I answered, annoyed with myself more than anything.

Archer came to my side, leaning down to pet Cora. "Let me guess, they don't do custom work with those sized windows?" he asked, a brow raised.

"Pretty much. Mostly because I want the best when it comes to these windows because I wanted them to last. But apparently I was mistaken."

Archer frowned, walked up to the glass panes, studied them, and cursed under his breath. "This looks like someone used either a glass cutter or an actual fucking diamond against them, Killian."

I froze, not liking how my name slid over his lips. Or the fact that he was saying someone had done it on purpose, something that was starting to worry me.

Because this wasn't the first thing that had broken in my house.

"I don't know who would do it, it's just me up here." Cora barked, and I grinned. "Me and Cora."

Archer smiled sadly, then looked up at the glass. "I would take some pictures for your insurance company, and hell, maybe call the police."

I stiffened and walked up to him. "The police?"

"If it's vandalism, it's good to know, especially if your neighbors want to sell over here."

I sighed. "Well, that's not what I wanted to hear."

"Our company can do this, by the way," Archer put in, and I blinked.

"Looking for sales?" I asked, teasing. Where the hell did that teasing note come from?

"Always. Though, right now, we're a little busy," Archer added with a laugh.

"And I take it glass work isn't your area?"

"Honestly, my twin Annabelle would be the best at it. She's the architect, and between her and my other sister, Paige, they know how to handle nearly everything."

"Do all of you guys work together?" I asked.

"Yep. One big happy family," he added, his voice a little strained.

I didn't want to ask, so I didn't. Instead, I looked at the glass and took photos.

"I'll think about the police, but I will take these photos for the insurance company." I paused, letting out a breath. "Thank you."

"No problem. And if you are looking for someone, I can ask my family. Or we can do it for you. It's what we do."

"I guess I'll need references."

Archer laughed at that. "Yeah, we can do that."

"I mean, if you're just out here going from house to house offering your services, you're probably going to need references."

His blue eyes filled with laughter. "You're right. Totally right."

"What are you doing out here anyway?" I asked, surprising myself.

Archer looked at me then, and I ignored those blue eyes. I had to.

"I'm just having a day. Wanted some time to think."

"Okay."

"You're not even going to ask?" Archer asked, then shook his head. "You shouldn't. It's kind of boring."

"I wasn't going to ask. It's not my business. And I don't really care."

Archer blinked, and I knew that last part had been a lie, and rude, but it was my best defense mechanism to get people to stay the fuck away from me.

"Well, since you didn't ask, I'm going to tell you. My ex is getting married. My mother asked me to head the family reunion for all one hundred Montgomerys because I have no life. Everybody else has a family, and I have no one. So, I wanted to feel sorry for myself in the mountains."

I just looked at him then and laughed. Because damn, I would love to have something so trivial be my issue. They might not be insignificant to him, but just then, I didn't fucking care.

"Seriously? You're sad because your family is getting married and having kids, and you aren't? And that your ex is getting married. You already told me that you didn't like him. That you didn't care. And now you care, and you need time alone to yourself? Pull your head out of your fucking ass."

I hadn't meant to say the words, and honestly, they weren't even for him. They were for me. I knew it. But by the way that Archer paled and took a step back, I knew I needed to be better.

"Shit. I'm sorry, Archer. I'm having a day, and I didn't mean to take it out on you."

Archer held up his hands. "No, I'm sorry. You're right. I know I need to get my head out of my fucking ass. I'm trying to. And I don't even know why I told you. You clearly don't want me to be here."

"*I* don't even want to be here, Archer."

"Why? Why are you here, Killian? Sure, I'll get my head out of my ass, and I will do it right now because frankly, I don't want to be the guy that a hot, grumpy guy in the woods yells at. But what's wrong? Why are you here?"

I could have said nothing. I could have walked away, punched him in the face, done anything other than say anything.

But I was just so tired.

"You want to know why I'm here? Because Cora is all I have left. Because I used to be a dad and a husband, I had that life that you are so jealous of."

The words tumbled out of me, and it was as if the world dropped from beneath my feet. The past rushed back like a slap in the face and my hands went clammy, my face losing all heat and color. I couldn't breathe, couldn't think.

I couldn't stop.

Archer moved forward. Froze. His eyes went glassy, his mouth parted like he wanted to say something, then stopped, then started again. "Shit, Killian, I'm sorry. You don't have to say anything. We can walk away right now and forget this happened."

That was the problem. I couldn't forget anything happened. Here I was, trying to live my life when at one point, I didn't even have a life to live, and there was no going back.

So the words escaped me, and I let them.

Finally.

I let them.

"No, I'll say it. I don't say it often, so I should say it to you."

I wasn't sure that even made sense to me, let alone Archer, but he was quiet and let me speak.

I didn't know whether to yell at him or thank him for letting me.

"I had the perfect wife. Danielle was amazing. She was kick-ass, smart, brilliant, worked hard, and the chemistry we had? Off the fucking charts. I couldn't keep my hands off her. And she loved it."

Archer again stood there, his face pale, his emotions etched on his face, but he let me speak.

So I continued, even as my heart shattered into a thousand new shards. "Our kid? Cassidy? She was the best thing in my life. From the first moment I held her, I knew that I wanted to be the best girl-dad ever. She was a daddy's girl through and through. She followed me around, helped me with my work. I used to be a carpenter. I used to build furniture and custom pieces for homes like this. That was my job. I used to wear the flannel, dirty jeans, dirty boots, and I worked. My wife ran a Fortune 500 company, worked long hours, and came home to a meal that I cooked, and a little girl that loved us both and laughed like nobody's business."

Archer's eyes watered, and he reached forward, but I took a step back. If he touched me, I'd break, and I was already on the precipice. "You do not have to continue this, Killian."

"Let me," I ground out, my voice breaking.

"Okay. Anything you need. Anything."

"Cora was a puppy. We left her at home that night since we couldn't take her to the dinner at the ranch. Dinner ran late with Danielle's family, and we were trying to drive home in the ice and snow, even though we shouldn't have. We were up in Wyoming, trying to get back down here. We were trying to get home, trying to get to the damn dog."

Cora whined, and I cursed again and rubbed my hand down her flank. It wasn't her fault. I knew that. I knew exactly whose fault this was.

"We hit black ice. Like everyone fucking does, only we were on a curve, with a car coming that *also* hit the damn black ice. We were next to an embankment, next to a lake."

"Killian," Archer whispered, his voice breaking.

I continued as if I hadn't heard him. "The car slammed through the ice. I don't remember much after that. Only the cold, so fucking cold. And Danielle's scream and Cassidy yelling, 'Daddy!' before we hit."

I sucked in a breath.

"The next thing I knew, I was on my back, somebody banging on my chest trying to get me to breathe, and it was so cold, and people were screaming. Sirens were screaming, and I turned to the left, wondering how the hell I could survive that, trying to get back to my family." Tears fell now, and my chest felt as if someone were carving it with a knife. "Cassidy was there. Her little body right next to mine, and she was so blue. So fucking blue." I met Archer's gaze, the horror in his eyes. "She was gone. They weren't working on her anymore. And I shouted, my voice hoarse, and I was going into shock, but I screamed for them to help her." I gulped in air. "I didn't know where Danielle was. I didn't realize 'till later that they still hadn't even gotten her out of the fucking car."

I wiped my hands on my pants and tried not to throw up. I barely held the bile down.

"My little girl was dead right next to me, and I couldn't even reach her, didn't even have the fucking energy to be the man I needed to be to get up and save her. She was dead. And my wife was gone, and there was nothing I could do."

I let out a sob, then sucked it in. I couldn't break anymore in front of this man. This damn *stranger*.

"Killian." Archer was crying now, moving forward, but I did my best to ignore him. I wasn't sure I could stand any longer if he touched me, if he told me how tragic it all was and how sorry he was. No words had helped before, and I wasn't sure if any words, from this man or anyone, would ever help me at all.

"There's nothing you can say. They're gone. So, I don't know if I'm the right kind of person to tell you what's good or not, to tell you what you're supposed to want. Because I had all that and I lost it. So maybe you're better off watching from the outside in. Because I sure as hell don't want you to ever feel this."

I couldn't believe I had said the words, I hadn't meant to say them at all.

I could barely feel anything, could barely do anything. Instead, there was just a jagged shard of ice sliding through my heart, one painstakingly aching moment of time trapped there forever.

And then Archer was there, his arms around me, and Cora was pressing against my side, and the man I had just shouted at was hugging me.

When was the last time I had been hugged like this?

I didn't want to think about it. *I couldn't.*

But Archer was running his hands up and down my

back, soothing me, muttering nothing and maybe everything.

After the initial sob, I had no more tears left, but I did the unthinkable. I slid my hands up his back and held him tight, my hands fisted in his shirt. I beat on his back, once, twice, and Archer didn't move, didn't let out an oof, didn't make a sound. Just held me.

After a moment, I felt the heat of his breath against my neck as he pulled away, but he didn't let me go. Instead, he looked at me and let out a breath.

"I'm sorry. That you went through that, that you're still going through that. I can't imagine what you're feeling, but thank you for trusting me with your family. For trusting me with you. And I'm so sorry that I keep encroaching on your space when all you want to do is be alone. I get that. Let me know what you need. Or nothing. I could walk away right now."

I wasn't sure what to say, but he was there, holding me, the first time I'd been held in years, and I almost felt okay.

Maybe not okay, but maybe a little more solid than I had been before.

I pulled away slightly, my arms moving, and then I was cupping his face, wondering why he was so warm when all I felt was the cold.

"Why are you still here?" I asked, but it wasn't to him. It was to myself.

His eyes widened and I couldn't think, I just lowered my lips to his, and brushed them once, twice, and then I got angry, pressing harder, teeth against teeth, lip against lip, and as I pulled away, my chest heaving, I gagged, shaking, Cora barked around us both as I put my hands on my knees, and bent down.

"Are you okay? It's okay. I'm here. You didn't do anything wrong, Killian. You're just breathing."

I had done *everything* wrong. Didn't he see that? "I need to go."

"This is your home. I'll go. I'm sorry."

I could feel him beside me, but I couldn't look at him. I had just kissed him. After talking about my dead wife and daughter, I kissed him.

What kind of man was I?

And when Archer left, my legs shook, and I let him go.

I fell to my knees, Cora pressing against me. I did one more thing I hadn't meant to do.

I wept.

Chapter Nine

Archer

"I still find it weird not to have the babies with me," Annabelle said as she sank onto the couch, her glass of wine sloshing slightly in the over-large cup.

I grinned as I looked at it, remembering the look on her face when I had bought them for her and Paige. There had been a Crate & Barrel sale, and I hadn't been able to help myself. Those goblets were about the size of my head, and every time they used them when I was at one of their places, it made me smile.

And after having to come here when I hadn't been in the mood because of a certain growly lumberjack guy, I needed the smile.

"That's what I was just saying," Paige said as she sipped her rosé. She practically had to put her whole face into the glass to get some, and I just snorted.

"You miss Emery then?" I asked, taking a sip of my water. I had plans to go look over the work that my team had done on the house today, so I wasn't going to drink. Plus, drowning my sorrows in alcohol probably wasn't the best idea. At least not today.

"Emery's with her daddy. So it's not like she's with a babysitter or anything. Lee is perfectly able to father his own child."

I just rolled my eyes as Annabelle grinned. "Jacob is with Hailey and Jack now. Of course, I may be holding myself back from checking the baby cam just to see what they're doing."

It didn't matter that Hailey and Jack were over two at this point, and Jacob had the kids many times during the week when Annabelle was out onsite and didn't want to leave them at the Montgomery daycare. Annabelle still had issues with not having her kids at her side at all times. I didn't blame her, since the twins were freaking adorable.

Benjamin and Brenna were the same way with Rafael, and Beckett and Eliza are that way with Lexington. I had the feeling that more babies would be added to the family, which would stress them more out about leaving them, sooner rather than later. I didn't know when my siblings were going to start trying again, but considering half of them hadn't tried the first time and they'd ended up parents, it could be any day now. I also knew that Beckett and Eliza were working hard on the adoption process for their next child, and I was excited for them.

The Montgomerys were growing day by day, and as I thought about the work that I had to do with the reunion, it just reminded me of the fact that, yes, there were way more Montgomerys out there than most people even knew.

"Okay, we need to stop talking about our kids," Annabelle said as she rolled her eyes. "Or work. Or cheese."

"What else is there?" I asked, my mouth dropping open. "Seriously. Why would you bring cheese into the conversation?"

Annabelle set her wine glass down and let out a sigh. "Because I think I have to stop eating cheese." Her voice broke, and while I knew she was overexaggerating, the shock made me nearly drop my glass.

"Cheese? You have to give up cheese?"

"Why? Is it your blood pressure? I know we eat a lot of vegetables and things, too, but I guess cheese isn't good for you."

Annabelle laughed. "Okay, you both need to stop this. Don't put down cheese."

The Montgomerys were addicted to cheese. We were practically born eating it. One did not take away a Montgomery's cheese.

"I'm having problems with my rosacea. And every time that I indulge in cheese, along with something else I have an allergic reaction to, I'm having issues. Not lactose issues," she cautioned, and I winced. "But skin issues. And it's not getting any better. It's getting worse. To the point that my meds aren't working." She pointed to a slightly raised area between her brows. "I've covered this up with makeup, which is not helping it, but every night now I have to do a cold compress on my face if I eat a lot of cheese. I think it's time to give it up."

I just blinked at her, then stood up quickly before sitting back down on the couch next to her and holding my twin close. "I'm so sorry. Is there anything I can do? Is there a dairy-free cheese we could have?" I asked, shuddering at the thought.

Paige leaned forward. "We can find something. Is it all dairy? Or just cheese?"

"I already quit drinking regular milk long ago. Lactose-free milk is the way for me. That, or oat milk. But I think it's time for me to go to dairy-free butter too."

"A moment of silence for the lack of Montgomery cheese in your life." I met Paige's eyes over Annabelle's head, and she winced.

"What?" I asked.

"Isn't that usually hereditary?" she practically whispered, and I shuddered.

"Dear God. And we're twins."

Annabelle shoved at me, even as she laughed. "It's fine. Once you stop eating it every week, you get over some of the withdrawals."

"I don't even know how to look at you right now," I teased as my phone rang.

I looked down at the screen and froze.

"Are you fucking kidding me?" Paige asked as she snatched the phone away from me. "He doesn't get to just call you."

"Is it Marc?" Annabelle asked, her voice ice.

I reached over my twin, plucked the phone from Paige's hands, and sighed. "Yes. And I'm going to answer because if I don't, he's going to call again, and it's going to bug me."

"Don't let him have any power over you," Paige warned.

I held up my finger, silencing them both, and answered. "Hello, Marc. What can I do for you?"

Annabelle's eyes narrowed at that remark, and I could have kicked myself. I hadn't meant to say that last part. I had wanted to sound calm and collected, like I didn't give a shit that my ex-husband was calling me out of the blue after he had sent me a wedding invitation and after the fact that I had kissed someone else who hated the fact that he had kissed me. Oh yes, and even with all of that, all I could do was think about Killian and not the asshole currently on the phone.

"Archer. I wasn't sure you would answer."

I stood up from my sisters as both of them reached for me. I waved them off and began to pace. They were going to want to know what was said anyway, so it wasn't like I could try to hide from them. But I also didn't want them to accidentally overhear anything Marc said. Oh, they would be able to hear my side of the conversation, but they wouldn't need to hear anything else.

"Well, you caught me on a good day." I cleared my throat. "Congratulations on your wedding," I said, surprising myself.

Both of my sisters clapped softly, and I figured I had sounded reasonable enough. See, I was taking the higher road.

Marc was silent for a moment before he cleared his throat. "Oh. I'm glad you got that. I didn't know how to warn you."

"Not quite sure why you would need to warn me. Or frankly, why you needed to invite me to your wedding." No, Marc just wanted me to know what was happening and hadn't had the balls to be anything but a dick about it.

"You don't need to come. I just, well, I figured we could be friends."

I rolled my eyes as both my sisters leaned forward on the couch.

"You don't need to do this, Marc."

"Now, Archer, don't be like that."

That got my hackles up. "No, you don't be like that. It's over between us. We had a dissolution of our marriage. Neither one of us owes each other a thing, not alimony, not phone calls. You are welcome to get married. In fact, you're doing it. Good for you. I'm sure you and Rebecca will be wonderful together. But this has nothing to do with me. You don't need to call me again. You don't need to worry if I'm going to come to your wedding and make a scene. Because I'm not part of your life anymore, Marc. And we both know I probably shouldn't have been before this."

"Archer. You know it's not like that."

"No, you don't know anything about what it should have been or what it is now. And I realize that now. I don't need you, Marc. And you did not need me. And that's fine. But don't call again. And don't wait for that RSVP card. I'm not going. Rebecca doesn't need to worry about me. Your family doesn't need to worry about me. And, Marc, you need to do what you've always done. Not worry about me. Goodbye." And with that, I hung up. I looked at my sisters, whose eyes were wide as they looked at me and clapped.

"Extraordinary," Paige said as she jumped up from the couch and practically threw herself into my arms. I rolled my eyes and caught her, hugging her tight, as Annabelle came to my side, squeezing me.

"I'm so proud of you, Archer. That was impressive."

I shook my head. "It was a long time coming."

It was odd, the relief sliding through me. I had been over Marc for a long time. And yet it felt new. Different.

I stood up for myself. Finally. Yes, leaving him in the first place had been a form of standing up, but not like this. Marc wouldn't call again. Because he wasn't going to get the reaction that he desired. I wasn't going to get a note about a baby, or another marriage, or an anniversary party. I wasn't going to get any of that because I wouldn't matter to Marc anymore because I wasn't someone he could manipulate.

I knew that now, and I hated the idea that it had taken me so long to figure it out.

In the end, I was okay.

At least, I was okay when it came to him.

I wasn't jealous of my sisters. I never really had been. But I had wallowed, and I didn't need to wallow anymore.

"Well, I know you'll want to get back up the mountain later today, so you're not drinking, so I will have a drink for you. Because I'm so darn happy for you." Annabelle kissed me on the cheek, then Paige did the same, and I held my sisters close.

"I love you both. Even though you guys got married and decided to find very hot bearded men on your own, I understand. You also made me an uncle, so I guess I'll let that slide."

Paige pulled back and glared. "You know, you do enjoy joking about the fact that you and Lee almost hooked up once. You're lucky I love you. Because I'm pretty sure that you're also Lee's type."

I snorted. "You know, there are a few ménages in our family. So we know that poly romances work well, but never for siblings. So don't you worry. Lee is safe from my clutches."

Paige laughed as Annabelle cringed. "Oh, good. Now there are images. Of you and Lee. Not Paige, and I don't know what to do with that."

I gave my best Grinch smile. "Oh, I have images too."

Paige pushed at me, and Annabelle cackled. "Oh stop,

you know that Archer and Jacob would've made a beautiful couple too."

Annabelle shrugged. "True. But I got there first. Sorry, you snooze, you lose." She wiggled her fingers at me, her eyes dancing.

I rolled my eyes. "It's true. Both of you picked the perfect men. Well, I guess I'll just have to keep on the lookout."

Both of them froze for a moment before they smiled softly in unison.

"So, you are looking?" Annabelle asked, not too innocently.

"Are you ever going to tell us what happened with this Killian?" Paige asked, leaning forward and fluttering her eyelashes.

My stomach tightened at the thought. "He's not for me," I whispered.

The girls gave each other looks before they turned to me. "What did we miss?"

"He has a lot of healing to do. He's been through so much. And this isn't one of those movies where I can heal him. He just needs time." *Or a way to turn back time.*

"I'm sorry to hear that. Well, if he needs a friend, you're a great friend," Paige put in.

"And if he needs a group of friends, we can be there for him. And I can promise you we will all be on our best behavior and not play matchmaker."

I gave Annabelle a look as Paige agreed with me.

"What? I'm serious. We don't push people on each other if they're in pain. We may tease, but we don't hurt. That's not the Montgomery way."

I moved forward and hugged her tight before I kissed her temple.

"I love you, twin."

"Love me, too!" Paige called out as she skipped towards me. I hugged them close together.

I loved my family, and I was doing exactly what Killian had told me to do. Getting my head out of my ass.

By the time I left our boozy brunch, I was late getting up to the project site. But I wanted to check through things before the team came back without me the next day, so that meant I had to go through my notes.

The fact that I probably should have come earlier today wasn't lost on me. However, I hadn't wanted to see a certain person. There, I said it. I was avoiding Killian. Because we had kissed. And then he had pulled away, breaking.

I pulled up to the house and looked at what had been done, nodding along.

My team was good, and I loved that I was putting my own stamp on this, not as part of the branch but as the leader. This wasn't something I thought I would ever be able to do, but Beckett had thought I'd be perfect for it, and since he was training Clay to do this as well, our family was changing the dynamics, at least when it came to work. I felt like I could finally do something.

I gave the house a quick survey before I pulled out my tablet and began to take notes, going over everything that had been done for the past couple of days when I had been on other sites working on plumbing jobs for Montgomery Builders. There were a few touch-ups that I wasn't one hundred percent happy with, so they would have to be at least fixed if not totally redone. It wasn't that it was bad, but I was a perfectionist, and people would just have to deal with me.

I moved around the house, doing my best not to turn and look in the direction of Killian's place. He needed time, space, and he did not need me.

And I had to be okay with that.

As if I had conjured him, Cora bounded towards me, barking a happy bark, and I set my tablet on the bench next to me and knelt down to pet the gorgeous golden Lab.

"Well, hello. I like this welcome."

I knew Killian was there. It was hard not to know he was there because I could feel his presence. But I did my best not to look up right away. Instead, I gave lavish praise and attention to the puppy in front of me before I forcibly pulled my gaze up to look at Killian.

He stood there, dark circles under his eyes, blond hair disheveled. His beard was coming in, but he needed to oil it or brush it or something. He looked unkempt, not groomed, and he shouldn't look sexy.

But dammit, he was like catnip to me like that.

There was something wrong with me.

"Hi," I said, surprised my voice sounded so calm, because I was anything but calm.

"You came back," Killian whispered.

I couldn't help but think about Beast saying that to Belle, right before Beast died and turned into an uglier version of himself. There was probably something inherently wrong with me that I had always found the Beast hotter than the human part of him, but I wasn't going to go down that path anytime soon.

"I did. Work."

"Yeah. Work." Killian cleared his throat, and that's when I noticed that his hands weren't empty. Instead, there was this little carving of a dog in play. I just blinked at it.

"Did you do that?" I asked, not knowing why I was even asking.

Killian nodded. "Yeah. I couldn't sleep, and I like to do things with my hands."

I met his gaze, and I saw the heat there before he banked it, and the fact that it mirrored mine worried me.

"Oh. It looks great."

I stood up, not realizing I had still been kneeling this entire time and moved towards him under my own volition.

"Is that Cora?"

"It is." Killian cleared his throat and handed it to me. "It's for you."

I nearly dropped it as I looked up at him. "What? Why?"

I cursed under my breath. "Not that I'm not thankful because it's amazing. The detail? I can't believe anyone could do this with their hands."

"I see the work you're doing on this place. You have skills, too."

Again, the innuendo, but I ignored it.

"Nothing like this, though. This is beautiful, Killian. But I'm confused. Why did you make this?"

Killian looked down, steeled himself as his jaw tightened. "To say sorry." He looked up at me.

I looked at those eyes as ice washed over me. "This better not be for the kiss," I blurted, hating myself, but I needed to say this. I did not want to be the one that got kicked again. "Don't give me an apology carving made with your own hands for the kiss. Please."

I deserved better than that.

"It's not," he growled out, his jaw tense. "Because I yelled. And I was an asshole. I'm an asshole a lot, but you didn't deserve it after all that. You let me speak my truth, and then we kissed. I didn't handle it well, and I'm sorry for that."

Killian moved forward then, and I looked up at him. "Oh. You didn't have to do that."

Killian looked at me then and reached out, sliding his finger along my jaw. "I think I did, Archer."

And then he lowered his mouth to mine, and I knew I was making a mistake that I wasn't going to walk away from.

Chapter Ten

Killian

Archer tasted of coffee, creamer, and something new. I groaned into him, wondering what the hell I was doing before he pulled away.

I swallowed hard and looked at him, knowing I'd taken a leap and possibly made a mistake.

Again.

This was not me. Archer had been the first person I had kissed since everything had changed. And now here I was, doing it again without even fucking thinking.

Maybe I needed to not think.

"I didn't expect that, but I guess that means that you're

not sorry about the kiss before." Archer tilted his head as he studied my face.

I stuck my hands in my pockets, swallowing hard. "I'm not sorry. About either. But I also don't know what I'm doing."

Archer's lips lifted into a small smile. "I never know what I'm doing either. I guess that helps."

"Maybe." I cleared my throat. "So, what are you working on today?" I asked, trying to keep up with my thoughts and emotions. I wasn't doing a good job of it.

Archer gave me a look and shook his head. "I'm going through everything that my crew did when I was on other projects. Just making lists and figuring out what I'm going to do tomorrow when I come up and work."

"So, you have other projects then?"

Archer frowned. "Do you really want to know this? Or are you trying to figure out exactly what just happened between us?"

I looked at him then, aware that Archer had found a strength, and had healed more since we last spoke.

Since I had yelled at him and told him to get over himself. I had been an idiot who had thought that only my pain mattered.

I had been so self-centered, something I had been for far too long because I couldn't imagine anyone else feeling the slice against their soul like I had.

And that was selfish of me. Something Danielle would've hated. Something Cassidy would've hated.

"I don't know what I'm doing, Archer. I'm just trying not to be the asshole that I clearly am."

Archer's lips twitched again, and I tried not to think about kissing them.

"Okay then. I am the lead plumber for Montgomery Builders, as you know, so yes, I'm working on a bunch of projects for my family. For me," Archer corrected.

"Are you the lead or the sole Montgomery on this project then? Are you considered a contractor?" For someone building their own house, I should have been better with the terminology, but getting lost in my head day-in and day-out wasn't always conducive to that.

Archer looked embarrassed for a minute, and while I didn't know what I had said to make that happen, I wasn't proud of it.

"Yes. I'm trying to branch out. I have the certification, but this has always been my brother Beckett's sort of thing."

"And now you're wanting to do it, too?"

Archer nodded slowly. "Yes. I'm good at it." I liked the sound of confidence in his voice.

"Does your brother not like the fact that you're doing this?" I asked, trying to understand the family dynamic.

"He's proud of me. He'd be out here in a minute if I needed help."

"That's good then." I wasn't sure what else to say. I mean, what do you say to a man you found attractive, kissed, and pushed away with alarming regularity?

"My family's pretty amazing. I'm lucky that way."

I held up my hands, knowing this was a powder keg of a conversation now, thanks to my blow-up last time. "It's good you have them. And that you realize that."

"Anyway, I'm just working." Archer leaned forward and rubbed Cora some more.

"She likes you," I said after a minute.

The other man just smiled. "Looks like."

And it seemed that I was starting to like him too. That could be a problem.

"I do have a question," Archer said after a minute, and I blinked.

"Yeah?"

"Did you kiss me just now because you wanted to say that you were sorry? Or to prove that you weren't?"

I pressed my lips together, then let out a breath. "I kissed you just now because I couldn't think about not kissing you. And that felt like the right thing to do at the time, even though it doesn't make any sense."

"Okay," Archer said after a minute.

"Yeah. I'm not the most eloquent."

Archer shook his head. "I think you're far more eloquent than you think."

"I don't know."

"Did you want to show me the rest of your house?" Archer asked, and I didn't know if he was leaning in for another kiss or if he was truly interested.

The fact that I didn't know should worry me, but then again, I was still figuring out exactly what I wanted.

And Archer confused things.

"Yes. I'll show you."

"Okay." Archer swallowed hard, and I tried to ignore the long, lean lines of his neck.

Maybe it'd been too long since I had been with someone. It had been years. And there was just something about Archer.

I needed to turn away, to walk away from him. To hide in my solitude like I had been doing for years.

But this man was making it hard.

And I couldn't help but remember Penny's words as she told me to find something worth living for. Even if it was just a moment in time to just breathe.

I showed Archer around my house, and he asked questions.

"Did you find someone to replace the windows?" he asked as we looked over at my boarded-up large bay windows.

"No, I was going to ask you, and then things...just happened."

Archer smiled. "Things do tend to just happen, don't they?"

I swallowed hard as my gaze went straight to his lips and told myself I needed to stop that.

"Do you want to help? I mean, give me the information."

Archer nodded and pulled out his phone. "This is the company that we use. I can get you a discount through

Montgomery Builders, though."

"Why would you do that?"

Archer was silent for long enough that I was afraid that I'd once again said something I shouldn't. "I don't know, Killian. It's not that I feel sorry for you, because I don't."

"Then why?"

The other man let out a low breath. "Because maybe I need a friend. And I think you do, too. Silly. I know."

"I'm not good at this, Archer."

"I'm not good at this either. Whatever the fuck this is."

My lips twitched. "I don't know what's going on. Other than yes, I could use help with the windows."

"This place deserves fantastic work. So I'll help you make them perfect, and hopefully we can figure out exactly what happened to them."

"I don't know if we will. But I don't like seeing them boarded up like this."

"Then we'll fix them. We're good at what we do."

I looked around the area, something light on my chest, not as heavy as usual. "So, your reviews online say—"

"You looked me up?" he asked, teasing.

Somehow I smiled. I didn't mean to. My cheeks hurt, and I rubbed them, wondering why on earth this felt so awkward, beyond the obvious.

Archer looked at me then as if he were following my thoughts, and his smile went a little sad for a moment before he continued asking questions about the house.

I wanted him to see this, to see what I was working on

and how much effort I was putting into it, even if it was for only myself.

It should feel wrong, shouldn't it? That I was showing a place that wasn't for him. That had been for Danielle and Cassidy. And Cora. But Cora was asleep in her doggy bed in the house, and I was standing here with Archer as if he belonged here.

Maybe it was just because Archer saw this place as something he could work on, so why did I want to kiss him again?

"If you keep looking at my lips like that, we're going to have a problem," Archer whispered.

I pulled my gaze away from his mouth, unaware I'd even been doing it.

"Should I say I'm sorry?"

And then Archer was moving forward, tracing his fingers along my jaw.

"You don't have to be sorry. But I also don't want to hurt you by being here."

"There's not much left of me to hurt, Archer," I muttered, surprising myself with the honesty.

"I think it's okay if you want a moment. I don't want to be the person that makes you do something you regret."

I didn't want him to feel that, and fuck, I didn't want to feel that way either. "I already told you that I don't regret kissing you."

"No. You said you weren't going to say you're sorry. I don't think that's the same thing."

"Okay. So, what should I do now?"

"That's not something I can answer."

"I don't know. Honestly, there's just something about you. And that should worry me."

"Same here. I'm not up here looking for anything like this. Whatever this is."

I looked at the other man, considered his words, and ran my hands through my hair. "I'm not up here for anything. Just solitude. But then Cora barks and reminds me that I'm not alone, and Penny shows up, and now you. I'm never alone."

At those words, something broke inside me, as if ice was cracking over the large crevice above my soul.

It was so loud, echoing within me. How could Archer not hear it?

"I came up here just to breathe, to figure out what I wanted," Archer said after a minute.

"And did you figure out what that was?" I asked.

He shook his head. "No. But I don't mind kissing you." He took a step forward, and I found myself pressed against the counter. The edge of the granite cooled me through my shirt, the line hard but kept me in the present. It was what I needed with him so close to me, my dick pressing hard against my jeans and, based on the long line at the front of his pants, he felt the same.

"I take it you like being the aggressive one?" I asked, only kind of teasing.

I was fucking teasing? Who the hell was I? Maybe I had been drinking and I hadn't even realized it. Because I shouldn't be teasing. But I needed to live in the moment, and all I wanted to do was lean forward right then and taste him again. To run my fingers down his body, to feel the softness or roughness of his skin.

"Aggressive? Hmm. Not always. I used to be." Something flashed over his eyes, and I wanted to ask, but I didn't want to break this moment.

Because I wasn't sure I would ever come back to this. Or *could* come back to this. "Tell me to stop."

This was the moment. The moment we could walk away and never think about this again.

"What if I don't want to?" Archer studied my face, his blue eyes going dark. "So we don't hurt each other, we'll just see what happens?"

"And no words. Because I don't know what to do or say, Archer." That might be a copout, but I didn't want to think. I just wanted to *be*.

He swallowed hard, and I knew he was thinking, going through his own shit, and I didn't know what to do.

So I leaned forward, and although I was the one to kiss him first, he kissed me back harder, with more need. His hands tightened on my shoulders, then slowly slid down my arms, gripping my hands before pressing me back against the counter.

There was nothing sweet or romantic about this. Not when our breaths were catching, our teeth were clashing, our lips pressing firmly against one another. I was tugging at his shirt, and he was doing the same to mine.

My fingers dug into the soft skin of his back, his muscles tensing under my hold. He leaned down, bending over to lick my nipple, tugging it into his mouth. My cock twitched, aching enough that I could feel it pulse inside my pants. When he bit down, I gasped, then he went to my other nipple, my hands sliding over his body as I tried not to come in my jeans.

I couldn't help but groan, needing him, wanting him as he moved up to kiss me again, and we panted into one another.

My cock pressed hard against the seam of my jeans, so fucking hard. I hadn't been this hard in way in too long. I was only used to my own hand, pumping myself until I came into my sheet, into my shower, ignoring the guilt at my own body's needs.

But I couldn't feel guilt right then.

It wouldn't be fair to him.

And, hell, it wouldn't be fair to me either.

"Tell me to stop," Archer whispered against my lips, and then again against my neck.

I didn't tell him to stop.

Instead, I just let myself be, and I didn't speak at all.

I licked against his lips and then his neck. His lips went to my chest, over the sparse hair there, and then he was sucking at my nipple, hard, harder than I was used to.

My dick went harder, and I swallowed, trying to catch my breath. I slid my hands through his hair, over his shoulders. And then he stood back, studying me, so I did the same, wanting to take him all in.

He was all muscle, lean, with ink down his arms, chest, and back.

He was gorgeous, one of the most stunning creatures I had ever seen.

He stepped closer again, until we were pressed together, chest to chest, skin to skin, and I sucked in a breast, shocked at the sensation.

"Too much?" Archer asked, and I shook my head.

"Just new."

Archer froze, his eyes wide. "Is this the first time?" He let out a breath. "I mean, the first time you've been with a man?"

I shook my head, touched that he would ask and be careful. "No. I've been pansexual my entire life." I trailed my hand over his jaw, his beard rough against my skin.

"Same here. I just, I didn't know exactly how far you wanted to go." He licked his lips and I was memorized.

"I think us keeping going is a good thing."

Whose words were these? I didn't know, but I didn't regret them.

Archer's gaze went to my lips, and I had a feeling he knew what I was thinking now. "What do you like?"

"I don't know anymore." And that was the most honest thing I could have said, and Archer seemed to appreciate it.

"Okay then. So do you like this?" Archer asked as he kissed me softly, gently, as if he were testing.

I nodded. "I do. Do you?"

Archer smiled softly. "I do. What about this?" He reached down and cupped me over my jeans. I groaned, and Archer chuckled roughly.

"I'm going to take that as a yes."

"How about a hell yes?" I whispered.

"Okay. What about this?"

He undid the fastening of my jeans and slid his hand underneath the waistband of my boxer briefs.

I moaned and nearly came in his hand, my cock twitching under his attention.

"Yes. Damn yes."

"Good. Really good." Archer's breaths were coming in pants, and that was just from him touching me.

What would happen if I touched him? I didn't realize I was already doing it. His warm, soft flesh was in my hand before I even took my next breath.

"Okay. Now that we know we both like that," Archer groaned out.

"Yeah?" I whispered, stroking him from base to tip.

"Yes. That, that's fucking amazing," Archer whispered. "What about my mouth? Do you want my mouth on you?"

"Only if I can have my mouth on you."

Archer grinned, his gaze going darker. "You're much better at this than you pretended to be."

I licked my suddenly dry lips. "I'm a little rusty."

"Well then. I'm enjoying learning together."

He cleared his throat, both of us slowly stroking each other off. "What about further?"

I shrugged, and at Archer's look, I finally answered. "It's been a while, and even before, I was usually the top."

Archer gave me a wicked grin. "I like doing both. So that's good to know."

"So today, if we continue, you don't mind being bottom?" I asked, feeling as if I were having such a surreal experience I could barely keep up.

Archer grinned. "I don't mind. Really."

"Good to know."

"However, I don't have a condom, as I wasn't prepared for this, so we may just have to be okay with the touching."

I grimaced, my face heating as I slowly lifted my hand from his dick. He did the same, and I only barely held back a whine. "Actually, my well-meaning neighbor might've already thought of this."

The other man's eye's widened as I reached around him into the kitchen drawer and pulled out a new box of condoms, unopened and ribbed for his pleasure.

"I think I love Penny."

I did too, but right then all I wanted was to let my gaze greedily roam all over him. "Apparently, she is a psychic and not just a hippie."

"That's good to know. Okay. I'm going to kiss you again since my hand is about to be on your cock again, and then we're going to see what happens."

"I'm all for that," I whispered, and then his mouth was on mine and he was squeezing the base of my cock.

Somehow our pants were off, our shoes tossed into a pile, and he was on his knees in front of me. He gripped my thighs, and the sight of him, his dark head in front of my dick, his lips right above the glistening tip, nearly sent me over the edge.

When he squeezed me, I closed my eyes, willing myself not to come. I didn't want to embarrass myself, but it had been so long since another person touched my dick, and here Archer was, expertly cupping my balls and hollowing his mouth over the crown of my cock.

He hummed along me, and I froze, doing my best not to shake.

"Grip the edge of the counter, don't fall."

I did as he ordered, and then his mouth was on me fully, and I was groaning, pumping my hips as I fucked his mouth, and he expertly gave me one of the best blowjobs I've ever had in my life.

He was by far the best man I had ever been with.

Archer continued to swallow me, and I reluctantly pulled away, my balls tightening, and covered the tip of my dick, squeezing.

"I don't want to come in your mouth. I'm not as young as I used to be. I don't recover as fast as you will." There was a slight age difference, less than ten years. It sometimes felt like I'd lived a thousand lives, and yet right then and there it didn't matter.

Only that I couldn't come more than once in a row, and I damn sure didn't want to fuck this up.

Archer grinned as he looked up at me, down on his knees, looking so perfect. I was fucking terrified. He stood up, and I cupped his balls, squeezing his dick, as I pumped him, once, twice, and he let his head loll back, groaning.

"Killian..." He licked his lips and I leaned down, kissing him hard before pulling back.

"This isn't exactly how I thought about christening the kitchen, but I don't mind," I whispered, as I rubbed our dicks together, another friction, a sensation that made my toes curl.

"Oh, I could do this again, and again, and again," he whispered.

"And what about now?" I whispered, reaching around and spreading him.

"Lube, fuck. I forgot lube."

"Hold on, I have that too," I mumbled, and as Archer began to laugh, I pulled out the bottle of the lube that sat in my kitchen drawer, and even though *I* had been the one to buy this, it had only been for solo use. But now it was going to be for something more.

I opened the bottle, squeezed some onto my fingers, and as I met Archer's gaze, worked us both.

He groaned before leaning down so his forehead was on my shoulder. We continued to rub against one another as I readied him. And then we were kissing, both of us moving against one another.

The sound of the condom opening forced my eyes open, and then he was running his fingers along the tip of my dick and rolling the condom over my length.

I groaned, my shaft pulsing as Archer moved to the counter, adjusting us so he was bent over slightly, and my condom-clad cock was sliding over his lower back.

"Is this angle going to work?" he asked, looking over his shoulder at me.

I rasped and leaned forward, stroking his cock. "Yes. It's going to work."

And then I was spreading him, slowly easing my way inside him.

He was so tight, and I was already far too hard.

We went achingly slow, both of us taking in deep breaths as we worked against one another. I didn't want to hurt him. No matter what, I couldn't hurt him.

Not with what he was doing for me.

He was so damned tight, and I was nearly afraid I would be too big for him. So I pulled out, rubbed his prostate over and over with my finger until we were both shaking before I moved again. Then I was deep inside him, and both of us still doing our best to catch our breath.

And when I began to move, Archer groaned, pushing back into me.

He wasn't looking at me. I could only see the strong muscles of his back, the tattoos that I finally let my tongue follow as I moved.

I wanted to see his face when he came. I needed to. I

needed to see his cock, and not just his back, so I pulled out and tumbled us both to the ground over our shirts and pants. It was uncomfortable, the wood pressing into my knees and his back, but I met his gaze and pressed deep inside again. And then we were moving, both of us grunting, lips against lips, skin against skin.

It wasn't pretty. It wasn't dainty. It was anything that I'd had before.

Instead, it was the two of us, needing one another and finding our rhythm.

When my balls tightened, I quickly gripped his dick again, pumping, loving the way that his mouth parted, his eyes going dark, and when he spurted all over his chest and stomach. I groaned, whispering his name and unintelligible thoughts as I filled the condom deep inside him.

And then I hovered on top of him, trying to breathe, and it was Archer who reached up and wiped the tears from my face.

They weren't for what he thought they were. He had to know that.

Because I didn't regret this.

I was just becoming okay with this.

Because there was no comparison.

But I didn't think that's what Archer saw.

Instead, he saw me still deep within him, crying over what he must think I thought was a mistake.

So I pulled out of him, trying to catch my breath because

I needed to tell him that everything was going to be okay. That I was going to figure shit out.

Archer swallowed hard and dressed quickly before I could do anything.

I reached for him, but he took a step back, his smile going wobbly and his own eyes glistening.

"Archer," I whispered.

He shook his head. "I have to go."

And then he was gone, shoes in hand, still sticky from what we had just done.

I sat naked on the kitchen floor, embarrassed, shaking, and knowing that while this hadn't been a mistake, it was hard to tell the difference.

Chapter Eleven

Archer

I blew out a breath, my cheeks inflating then deflating quickly. I had made some terrible mistakes in my life. Okay, perhaps not wholly awful, nothing horrific that would break me. But I had indeed made some mistakes.

My marriage had been a mistake, but I wouldn't go back and change it. I had needed to make those wrong choices in order to become myself.

I hadn't stood up for myself with Marc or my father until it had almost been too late. But I had lived through that, and while I didn't regret the choices I made, I still knew that they were mistakes.

I wouldn't allow myself to think of the mistake that

would cost me more than I could bear. The one that was going to cost me far too much.

A mistake that had everything to do with the man I shouldn't have wanted.

Killian had cried. He had *cried* after we had rough sex on a kitchen floor.

I let out a shaky breath, annoyed with myself for letting any of my emotions through. Why had I slept with him? Why had I put myself in that situation?

I sat around with my brothers, brothers-in-law, and my father, as we watched a hockey game, crossing our fingers that the Avalanche actually did something for themselves this year, and yet all I could do was get stuck in my own head because I had slept with a man I had hurt.

Oh, I might not have done it on purpose, but I had to have hurt him.

Because I had been selfish and I had wanted him.

And he had cried.

"What's going on in that head of yours?" Lee asked as he stared at me, studying my face.

I put on my best Archer Montgomery smile and winked.

"Just thinking about how I should have moved quicker when it came to you. But Paige stole you out from under me."

Beckett snorted from beside me. "Our little sister's going to beat you up one day if you don't stop joking about that."

"I don't know. I think the two of them would've been a cute couple," Jacob added as he sipped his drink.

Annabelle's husband was exhausted; I knew that he hadn't been sleeping. I wasn't the only one going through my own turmoil these days.

We had buried his mother eight months ago. She had remained on this earth for as long as possible with a smile on her face. She'd done so even as the ALS had progressed, so she could hold her grandchildren.

And eight months ago she had taken her final breath, with her husband, Jacob, and Annabelle in the room. I had been still living with them, watching over the twins as they tried to comfort each other in their grief.

It was hard not to wonder how selfish I had been for keeping my head up my own ass, as Killian had told me. Because other people were going through far more hell. Losing so much, and all I had lost were a few smiles along the way and part of myself, which I had freely given.

"Okay, that was a deflection if I ever heard one," Lee scolded as my brothers turned towards me, and my father raised a brow.

I shook my head. "I don't want to talk about it."

"Did Marc do something?" my dad asked, scowling.

"It wasn't Marc, I promise."

"But he called you when you were with the girls," my dad pushed.

I closed my eyes. "Sometimes, I swear our family is a little too close."

"Again with the deflection," Lee said as he punched my

side. I was still healing from the fall and then had re-bruised myself in the best way on that kitchen floor.

"Ow." I rubbed the spot where he had hit. "What was that for?"

"I didn't hit you that hard."

"You shouldn't be hitting me at all, right, Dad?" I asked, teasing.

My dad just rolled his eyes. "I'm not getting in the middle of that. You're adults. But if it's going to knock some sense into you," he began, and I rolled my eyes. Because my father had never once hit us. Oh, he had crossed a few lines professionally when he hadn't been able to cut the strings of his connection to the company, but he was still a fucking amazing dad.

"I can't believe you're taking his side. I'm your son."

"So is Lee. Get over it. He married into the Montgomerys."

"I'm not actually a Montgomery," Lee warned.

"Don't try to tell them that," Jacob put in. "They won't believe you."

"Because you *are* Montgomery. Get over it," Beckett said as he scowled at the Avs losing the puck. Again.

"Why are you even watching this? As soon as we lost Sakic, everything just went downhill," I grumbled.

My dad threw a chip at me. "Because we don't jump ship when things don't go well. And they have some amazing guys other than Joe Sakic—who we still love, but it's been how many years since he retired, Archer Montgomery? Get over it. Now, what's going on with you?"

I sighed. I knew I wasn't going to be able to get out of this anytime soon.

"I met someone." As the heat began to crawl up my neck and to my ears, my dad studied my face.

"Did he hurt you?"

I shook my head, even though that was a lie. Seeing those tears after Killian moved off me had hurt. But that was *my* problem. Not his. Because Killian hadn't been ready, I should have known that.

Hell, our first kiss was right after he told me he had lost his wife and child. After literally explaining to me that his wife and child had drowned and/or froze to death in a lake, we kissed. I was the selfish asshole here, and though watching the tears fall from Killian's face as I walked away had cut me like a jagged edge of a blade, it was still my fault. Something I needed to get over.

"Is it the mountain man?" Lee asked.

There were truly no secrets in my family. Not anymore. "Yes, the mountain man," I said with an eye roll.

"What's his name again?" Lee smiled at me, his gaze penetrating.

I swallowed hard. "Killian. His name's Killian."

"It's a good name," my dad said slowly as he looked at me. "And why is this man with a good name giving you such pause?"

I looked down at the now warm beer in my hands and

took a big gulp, ignoring the bitter taste, and my own feelings.

I had bottled everything up with Marc, not telling my family about everything that had happened—my family who were also my best friends—and where had it left me? Alone, damaged, partly broken, and afraid of my own failings.

Maybe I need to be better.

"I don't know if you're going to want to hear this part, Dad," I said with a wince as Benjamin chuckled softly from across the living.

"Do you need me to leave the room?" Dad asked, looking between us.

I closed my eyes. "No. I guess it's fine. Killian's been through some shit, and I went up to the place up in Boulder in order to just think and to work; and he's doing the same on his place."

"So, he's building a house then?" my dad asked.

"Yeah. It's pretty cool too."

"Is this the place with the windows that you talked about?" Beckett asked.

I nodded. "Yes. How's that coming along, by the way?" I asked.

"It's good. I've talked to the guy. He seemed growly but nice. So, I guess like a Montgomery," he teased.

I let out a slow breath. "Yeah. He's that, I think."

"So, what happened?"

"Anyway, I'm enjoying the work. I love the house. It's calling to me, you know?"

"You've always been good at more than just plumbing," my dad put in.

My hackles rose as everyone stared at my father, narrowing their gazes.

Dad held up his hands. "I'm sorry, I shouldn't have added the word *just* there. What I meant was you can do so many things. You're a master plumber, and you have your contracting license because you're talented. You could do any job at Montgomery Builders."

Lee snorted. "Probably not Paige's."

"I would be great at Paige's. I'm a people person."

"You are not a spreadsheet person, though," Lee countered.

I winced. "True. Thanks, Dad. Seriously, a compliment like that means the world to me, I promise you. But each of us is in the jobs that we should be in. I'm just having fun doing additional things with this house."

"And I like the fact that you come to us with any questions you have," Beckett put in.

"Because we all do that. We have our assigned roles and teams, but we also pitch in when needed. The fact that you're doing this as sort of a Montgomery Builders' branch right now is fucking amazing." There was a light in Beckett's eyes at that, and it stirred something within me, but I didn't have time to think about it then. Maybe later. I would hope later.

"Before I derailed us with the talk of work..." my dad put in. "What happened, son?"

I took another drink of my beer and set the glass down on a coaster. Annabelle would hate it if we left rings on her hardwood table.

"We fight a lot." I looked up at the other guys and held up my hands. "Not in that way. Not rudely. It's just...we butt heads and he makes me say things that I don't mean to out loud."

I laughed at the end of my sentence, and the twins shared a look while Lee and Jacob did the same. My dad just stared at me, his gaze intent. So I continued. "He told me why he's on the mountain." I let out a breath. "It's not my story to tell. Just know that it was utterly horrific, and I don't even know how he's still standing. And somehow, he trusted me with a part of him that I don't think he trusted with anyone else."

"That's something," Dad whispered.

"Maybe. Or it was. I don't want to get into too many details," I hedged, even though I had a feeling everyone in this room knew exactly where I was going with this. "However, one thing led to another, and I made a mistake."

Humiliation settled over me. The men in front of me might be my family, they also didn't judge me. I would forever be grateful for them.

"Did he hurt you?" Beckett whispered, leaning forward.

"You already asked that question."

"And we are asking again," Benjamin said.

"Not in the way you're thinking. It didn't work out. He wasn't ready, and frankly, I don't know if I am either." I let out a breath and looked down at my hands. The hands that have been over Killian's, the hands that had touched him. And the hands that had pushed away as Killian had fought for breath. "Either way, it was a mistake, and now I have to work on the mountain and avoid him, which I'm not very good at doing. He just wasn't ready. And I feel like I pushed him."

There, that was the truth. What hurt me the most. Not that Killian had pulled away before I had been able to, but that I had pushed at all.

"From what I know from the few times we've spoken, Killian doesn't seem like a man who would do something he didn't want to," Beckett put in slowly.

I shook my head. "He wasn't ready."

"Okay then, then find a way to make it up to him," Jacob put in.

I shook my head. "I think the best way for me to do that is by avoiding him completely and pretending that it never happened," I said quickly.

My dad let out a rough breath. "I think this is the first time any of you have ever come to me, or even allowed me in the room when you've had this kind of conversation," he said, the tips of his ears reddening. It was the same thing that happened to me just then, and it just reminded me of the fact that I was talking about sex without talking about sex with my father in the room.

I was losing my mind.

"Whatever happened, son, it was with two consenting

adults, and if you feel it was a mistake, and I'm not talking about Killian here, I'm talking about you. If you feel like it was a mistake and you never want to do what you did again, don't. But if you feel that you have guilt or something else washing over you that's pressing down on your shoulders, you need to talk to him about it." We all gave my father an incredulous look, and he shrugged.

"I didn't talk about what I was feeling for thirty years. And it screwed up so much in my life. I almost lost my wife, my kids, and everything else that's come from that. Don't be me. Talk. Even if it's just to apologize or to say that the slate is clean. Talk. Because Killian deserves it for sure, but Archer? You do too. You deserve that honesty." My dad cleared his throat then and gestured to the game. "We just missed a score. The Avs are up 2-1. I guess it is freezing in hell, with this score and the fact that I'm talking about my feelings with you," he said and held up his beer. "To the Montgomerys." He looked at his sons-in-law. "All of them."

Jacob and Lee just rolled their eyes, and we each held up our glasses.

"To the Montgomerys," I whispered, echoing the others, and I drank the last of my beer and leaned back against the couch as we changed the subject purposely to something a little bit lighter.

I had made a mistake, but maybe my dad was right. Maybe I should be the one to apologize. Or push things away, and pretend it never happened, but not avoid him.

I wasn't sure what I was supposed to do, but as I sat in

that room with my family, I realized that I had never been alone.

Killian had been right.

I was home. Not alone.

And that would just have to be okay.

Chapter Twelve

Killian

I frowned down at the address on my phone and tried to talk myself out of what I was doing. However, I had gone through the painstakingly long process of finding Archer's address, thanks to a friend.

Now I was standing in front of an apartment building in Fort Collins after leaving Cora with Penny. I had hated leaving her with Penny, and Cora had given me her sad puppy-dog eyes, and though she loved long car rides, I had needed this time alone to think. She was a great buffer between Archer and me. And I didn't deserve that buffer. I needed a moment to think and to just figure out what the hell I wanted.

My phone buzzed and I picked it up, answering, grateful for the distraction.

"Let me guess. You're standing outside of his apartment building, wondering if you should hold a boom box over your head?"

I smiled at Penny's words and shook my head even though she couldn't see me. "You know I only know what a boom box is because of that movie, right?"

"You haven't even seen it in full. You just know memes. Also, you are old enough to have seen it. You're not that much of a spring chicken."

"Did you somehow call me an infant and old in the same sentence?" I asked, Penny's words soothing me even though they didn't make much sense. I trusted her with my dog and was grateful that I could hear her voice—because it was somebody. Somebody that wanted to talk to me that wasn't Cora.

"I'm not sure I should go inside," I whispered.

"Of course, you should go inside. You need to grovel to that young man and explain to him that you are a good person who just had a bad day."

Although Penny didn't know everything that had happened, she knew enough. Had seen me standing there after I had cleaned up, my face pale, sweat slicking my back since I hadn't put my shirt back on.

She had seen me trying to make sense of everything, and not doing a good job of it.

"He's not going to want to talk to me. He walked away, remember?"

"I don't know exactly what happened in that kitchen, but in my not-spring-chicken ways, I can guess, Killian."

I winced. "Please don't guess."

She chuckled roughly, but I didn't smile. I was so fucking embarrassed. Not for Penny, but for the way that I had reacted. Because I had hurt Archer. I was here to apologize, but what more did I want beyond that? That was a problem. Something I probably should have figured out before I drove all the way the fuck out here.

"So, talk to me."

"What do you want to know?" I asked softly.

"What are you going to say to him?"

"Well, since you're calling, I was kind of hoping you had answers for me."

"Killian, darling. I may have the answers to the universe, but I don't have your answers here."

"That doesn't seem very fair."

"Then here's my answer. Life isn't fair, but you can find goodness. Especially if you let yourself be that goodness."

"You're very confusing, you know," I whispered.

"I know I am. But I'm that wise hippie woman in the mountains that shows up every once in a while with the good stuff."

I snorted. "It's legal out here now you know. You're not so out of the ordinary."

"I never was, child. I was extraordinary."

"You still are."

"See, that was a kind thing to say. Now, what are you going to say to him?"

"I'm currently standing in front of his building. I need to go up a flight of stairs and knock on his door. I hope to hell he doesn't close it in my face."

"Did you hurt him?" she asked, her voice low, but I wasn't sure if there was a warning in there or sadness. I wasn't sure which one I wanted to hear. "What do you want from him?"

"To say I'm sorry."

"If you didn't hurt him, not in that way, then what do you have to be sorry for?"

"Are you saying I shouldn't be sorry?

"I'm saying you should have a better answer than that when Archer asks. And you should have a plan. For example, do you want to see him again? Because driving an hour to him in the evening just to say I'm sorry when you don't want to see him again is kind of sending mixed signals."

"I haven't dated or been with anyone since Danielle. You know that, Penny."

Penny sighed, and I heard the hurt in her voice, even if she tried to hide it. "I know. You've been hurting yourself longer than anyone would ever think you should."

"I'm not hurting myself. I'm just living as who I need to be."

"That's a bunch of horse crap, and you know it. Danielle wouldn't want you to be like this. I didn't know her, but I know you enough to realize that you wouldn't have loved a woman that would want you to hurt this way. Live your life. Even if Archer is just for this mere moment of that life, if he brings you something other than profound sadness, then it is something worth trying for. And if tonight is just you apologizing and walking away, then that is something that you lived for. Something that you did. It's no longer you just going through the motions. But figure out what that is. I promise you it'll be worth it."

"I don't know how to do this, Penny."

"I never figured it out either. But you're the strong one, Killian. You can do it. And Cora is on my lap right now, agreeing with me. Good luck, Killian. I believe in you."

Cora barked, and I smiled before I hung up and sighed.

What should I do? I should probably have figured this out before I'd driven out here. I had the entire hour to think, but all I could try to formulate was how to say I was sorry for hurting Archer. I hadn't thought beyond that. Because my brain wouldn't let me.

My phone buzzed again, and I answered. "What is it, Penny? Do you have any more wise words for me?"

"I'm glad that you answer Penny's calls," Ann said, and I smiled at my sister's voice. Smiled. Actually fucking smiled. That was different for me.

"I'm answering you, aren't I?"

"Because you think I'm Penny." My sister let out a sigh, and I heard the emotion in the crack of her voice. "I'm just glad to hear your voice. That you're not up on the mountain alone."

"Or not on the mountain at all," I said casually, even though there wasn't anything casual about it.

"Where are you?" she asked, her tone on alert.

"I'm in Fort Collins. About to meet, well, a friend."

There was so much in that silence. I wasn't sure what I should have said.

"A friend."

"A friend, Ann. I'm just going to meet a friend."

"That's good," she said, her voice breaking.

"Ann. I was an asshole to this person, and I'm apologizing to them. I don't think it's what you think it is."

"Of course, you're an asshole. That's who you are. It's why I love you, big brother."

"I don't know how to take that."

"Well, you didn't yell at me or hang up, so I'm going to take it well for you. Now, go apologize, and have a friend. I love you so much, Killian."

"Ann," I whispered, so much in that one word that I wasn't sure what else to say.

"I'll talk to you soon."

"Why are you calling? It had to have been something. Is it the kids? The baby?" My stomach clenched, and I held my breath.

"I assumed I would just get your voicemail. We're all doing wonderful, Killian. And I just wanted to hear your voice. I miss you, you know. Dumbass."

My lips twitched, and my heart twisted just a little bit. I had pushed Ann away, knowing she had her family and had roots that she was putting down on her own. She didn't need me.

I had told myself I didn't need her.

"I'll call you back soon. And you can update me on the family."

"I would love that," Ann whispered, her voice full of tears now.

"Don't cry, Ann."

"I don't know who this friend is, and the fact that you were an asshole is probably not encouraging, but I'm going to take it as encouraging anyway. I love you, big brother. Now go grovel. You do a good grovel."

"Ann," I growled.

"Love you." She hung up and I shook my head, holding back a laugh.

I froze, rubbing my fist over my chest—an actual goddam laugh. I looked up to where Archer's apartment was and shook my head. "Who are you, Archer Montgomery?"

There was a catalyst for this change, and I wasn't sure I liked it.

But I needed it.

I put my phone in my pocket and went up the stairs, my chest aching from the speed of my heart as I made my way to Archer's apartment.

Maybe he wouldn't even be home. Maybe he was with his family. Or, fuck, maybe he was on a date.

I should have just waited for Archer to get back to the mountain and talk to him there. Or hell, I could have called him. Done anything other than stand out here in the cold wondering if I should actually knock on the door.

I let out a breath and told myself I just needed to not throw this away. To at least do this part. To take that step. Because I hadn't been *living* long enough, just surviving. Growling at myself while I worked on my house wasn't enough.

If it had been, then why was I even bothering with the mountain?

I banged on the door, emotion churning within me, making it a little more forceful than I planned on.

Archer opened up quickly, and his eyes went wide at the sight of me. "Killian? What the fuck?"

Archer looked like he hadn't shaved in a few days, his dark beard coming in nicely. His hair was slightly disheveled, and he had a warm gray Henley on, one that was just tight enough against his chest to show his defined muscles. He had pushed up the sleeves to expose his forearms and his ink.

He had on jeans, worn slightly around the pockets and knees, and there was a hole right at the edge of one seam, probably where he had run into something when he was working.

And he was barefoot.

I frowned, wondering why the sight of his toes did something for me.

Did I have a foot fetish I didn't realize?

"Killian? Are you okay? What's wrong? Is it Penny? Cora?"

I swallowed hard and forced my gaze up to him. "What?"

"You're staring at me. Hell, you're here." Archer took a step back and held up his arm. "Get in here. It's chilly. And I have neighbors that are nosy. They're all watching out of their doorbell cameras at this point."

I snorted and took a step in, grateful that he had even let me walk through the door.

"How did you find me?"

"I know people," I said, shrugging.

"Well, that's not creepy at all," Archer teased.

"Sorry. For just showing up. I probably should have called, texted, or done anything other than just showing up at your apartment."

I looked around the place, noticing it was tidy, with nice furniture, far nicer than something that should be in an apartment this small.

Archer seemed to follow my gaze and shrugged, stuffing his hands into his pockets. "I got to keep some of my furniture from the house after we sold it, and I haven't figured out what house I want next, so it's apartment living for now."

"Oh. I'm not judging. Seriously. You've seen where I live."

Archer raised a brow, and I swallowed hard.

This man. This man just did something to me. I should

walk away, should pretend that it didn't matter. Only it did. And that worried me. So fucking much.

But I had spent so much time in the darkness, hating myself.

Maybe I should just step out into the light. Because Archer had. I could try, too.

And where the hell had those thoughts come from?

"Are they okay, though? Is everyone else? If you're not here for them, why are you?" Archer asked as he rocked back on his heels.

I ran my hand over my hair and sighed. "I'm here to apologize."

Archer's face went stony, his jaw tightening. "Don't apologize. Whatever you do, just don't fucking do that."

I met his gaze then and then cursed under my breath. "Not for what happened. Fuck, never for that. I promise you. What happened was consensual, you know that. It was what I wanted."

"Really? I watched you cry afterward. As if you couldn't get away from me quick enough."

"You're the one that left!" I shouted and cursed again. "I'm sorry."

"No, I did leave. Because I couldn't watch you break because you had slept with someone for the first time since losing your wife. You love her, and I know that, and you probably always will. I'm never going to step in the middle of that. But, fuck, Killian, you were crying and we weren't even talking. It just happened, and suddenly we had our hands on each other we're fucking on your kitchen floor. Who the hell does that? Who the hell just rips off each other's clothes and fucks each other on the floor, except in a porn movie?"

"Well, we did. And we're not in a porn. That I know of."

Archer's blue eyes widened, his mouth parting. "You're joking. Who the hell are you, Killian? You don't joke."

"I don't," I said, throwing my hands in the air. "That's the problem. I have no idea who the fuck I am, and yet here I am standing at your door, trying to listen to my sister and Penny about how to grovel. I'm really not good at it."

Archer froze in front of me. "You talked to your sister and Penny about what happened?" he asked, a blush riding high on his cheeks.

I rubbed the back of my neck. "Not in so many words. Not in any words. More I'm here to say I'm sorry. For making you feel that you had to walk away. Because you didn't."

"You needed time to think, Killian. And so did I."

That sliced across my chest, but I nodded. "I did, but maybe we should have done that together. Maybe we should do the one thing that we are not good at and actually talk."

Archer looked at me then and gestured towards his kitchen. "Then let's do it."

I looked down at the kitchen floor, then at him, and Archer blushed again. "I meant talk. Like get a beer. We can sit on the couch. We're not going to have sex in my kitchen."

"I'm just clarifying," I joked.

"Another joke? What the hell is going on?"

"The hell if I know. One minute I am trying to build a house for the family that I don't fucking have anymore. The next, I'm catching you as you fall off a roof. And then right after that we're yelling at each other, and then sort of getting to know one another. And I'm bearing my soul to you, and then we're fucking on my kitchen floor. How the hell does all that happen?"

Archer just blinked at me, then moved past, and I ignored the woodsy scent of him as he reached into the fridge, grabbed two beers and popped their tops off.

"I think we need this."

"I'm good with that."

I clinked my bottle to his, and he raised a brow before I took a big gulp of mine. The hoppy brew slid down my throat and I sighed, then followed Archer into the living room.

He patted the cushion next to him on the couch, and I sank down into the dark leather, relaxing.

"Maybe I should get a couch like this."

"You don't have much in the ways of furniture except for the bed you said you got for Cora. This is a comfortable couch."

"Maybe I'll add it to my list."

"How long is your list at this point?" Archer asked.

"You don't want to know."

Archer shook has had. "That's the problem. I think I do

want to know. Because if you're here to apologize and for us to talk, maybe we should."

"You want to talk about my to-do list?" I asked, feeling as lost as ever.

"Maybe. Or just anything. Like, what is your last name."

I blinked and looked at him. "You don't know my last name?

"No. Does that make me the whore?" Archer asked, fluttering his eyelashes.

I narrowed mine. "Don't do that. Don't call yourself that."

"I was teasing. I don't think of myself that way."

I swallowed hard, my heart still racing. "Hart. My last name is Hart."

Archer smiled at me, then he swallowed hard, and I watched the way his throat worked. "It's a good name. A little ironic and on the nose."

"I can't help it. I was born with it."

"How do you spell it?"

"H-A-R-T. No E. Not the actual heart."

"So. You're here."

"Yeah. I am. I don't know what's happening, Archer. I don't know what I want, other than I've been on that mountain for three years, trying to hide from or find something in fucking life. And the moment that I see you, I'm suddenly speaking again and growling and cursing, but I'm talking to you."

Archer smiled then, and it went right to my chest. "I feel

like you did the same to me, just in a much more subtle way, since I'm not coming from the same abyss as you."

I shook my head, then reached out and gripped his hand. We both looked startled at the touch, but I didn't let go. "I'm sorry. For downplaying anything that you're going through."

"I'm sorry for thinking that I'm the center of the universe when there's more going on out there than me getting dumped and feeling like shit because of the way he treated me."

"I feel like I should find this ex of yours and punch him."

Archer just smiled and took a sip of his beer. "My siblings would be in line before you. I'm just saying."

"Good to know."

"So, what is it that you want, Killian?" Archer asked after a moment, and I looked down at our joined hands before I squeezed his and pulled away, just needing to think.

Archer seemed to realize that because he didn't look sad that I had pulled away, instead he looked like he was thinking as well.

"I don't know what I want. I do know that I'm a mess. A huge fucking mess that's going to need time to think and will make mistakes. But I'm not sorry for what happened in my kitchen."

"I'm the one who walked away. But I'm not sorry either," Archer muttered.

"That's good," I said. A severe understatement, since it

felt like the weight of a single world fell off my shoulders as five more piled on top of my chest.

"So, what happens now?" Archer asked.

I shook my head. "You tell me. I don't know anything about doing this."

"And what's this?"

"You're really going to make me say the D word?"

"I don't think you're talking about dick, are you?" Archer asked, grinning, his eyes twinkling.

I laughed, throwing my head back, my body shaking. "I meant dating."

"Oh. *That* D word. Well, I used to be good at it, at least I thought so, not so much anymore. I guess we can figure it out."

"So, what does that mean?"

"That means tonight I'm going to turn on my movie, we're going to watch Chris Evans walk around in very tight leathery spandex, and then I might kiss you before you go home."

"I could do that. I like Chris Evans."

"I was sure you would. Everyone likes Chris Evans."

I snorted. "And then what happens?"

"And then we go about our days, we work, and maybe we go out to eat. And maybe I tell you a bit more about my family. And maybe you tell me a bit about yours."

"And then what happens?" I asked, my voice barely above a whisper.

"And then we see where it leads us. We don't need a rule-book or a path. But I don't want to hurt you."

I looked at him and let out a shaky breath. "I don't want to hurt you, either. Because I don't know if I'm ready for anything beyond maybe this movie. And Chris Evans," I teased, trying to lighten the tension, even though it did nothing about it.

"I don't know if I am either. So we figure it out. Together."

"Together."

Then Archer turned on the TV and we watched Chris Evans smile at the screen and tell us he could do this all day.

And I had to hope that was a good omen for exactly what was going to happen next.

Chapter Thirteen

Killian

"I'm fucking nervous." I ran my hands through my blond hair as Penny snorted beside me. She took a long inhale of her joint and handed it in my general direction. I shook my head. "You know that's not my thing."

"I thought it would help with your nerves. You never know."

I just sighed and looked up to stretch my neck. "I don't think getting stoned before my date—the first date, mind you, that I've had in a decade or so—is probably a good idea."

"This isn't your first date. I assume your first date was a casual walk through the woods checking out the property.

Your second date was a beer and a movie at Archer's house. This is your third date."

I paused in the act of rolling up my shirt sleeves, since I had decided to wear a button-down with dark jeans, the gray shirt the only color I owned these days.

"Third date. You're going to go with that math?"

"I'll go with any math that makes it less nerve-wracking for you."

I smiled at the woman who had become my friend despite me doing my best not to let her be anywhere near me.

"You look nice, though. Good jeans, a crisp shirt. Although, in my day, a man would be wearing slacks."

I looked over at her and raised a brow. "In your day, you wouldn't be wearing a bra, and you'd be wearing a hippie skirt. Now, look at you in your lounge pants and tank top."

"Excuse me. I'll have you know I'm not wearing a bra underneath this tank top because it has a built-in."

I rolled my eyes and made sure that my wallet and phone were in my pocket. "I'm meeting him at the restaurant since it's in Boulder, and he has to drive far to get out here."

"An hour's not too far these days, but that is still a distance."

I raised a brow, then pet Cora, knowing she left dog hair all over my jeans. That was fine with me. I was used to it. "Maybe the distance is needed."

"So you're saying that a physical distance will help the

emotional version that you're putting between you two? Very cute with the metaphors."

"Maybe it's okay that I don't have all the answers yet. I haven't been good at getting them anyway."

"That is true. But look at you, going out on a date."

I rubbed my chest with my fist and let out a deep breath.

"Maybe I should just not go."

"If you disappoint that young man and hurt him, I'm going to have words with you. I will always be your number one supporter, Killian. But you need this just as much as he does."

"He really needs a broken old man?"

"There's nothing old about you, except perhaps your soul. And you're not broken. You're healing. Maybe with a little bit of duct tape and adhesive, but it's working."

"You have a lot more confidence in me than I do."

"Somebody other than Cora has to. But remember, that dog loves you and trusts you no matter what. Maybe you should let someone else do that."

The L-word just then made me want to vomit, but I didn't say anything. Instead, I leaned forward, kissed her on the top of her head, and said goodbye to Cora.

"I need some time."

"You've had nothing but time, Killian. It's okay to just want to be in the moment."

"And figure out exactly what I'm doing with this guy."

"Or boy, basically."

"I keep calling myself an old man, and you keep calling him a boy. It's starting to creep me out."

"Then maybe you should stop calling yourself old. You're young, not carefree in the slightest, but you're allowed to make new memories, to breathe, and to believe. Just have faith in yourself."

"We both know that's not going to happen."

"Then have faith in the promises that you made."

"That's what you say."

I kissed her on the forehead again, and then I ran, out of breath, to my truck.

It was getting colder at night, but that was fine with me. I needed the stiff breeze against my skin as I tried to catch up with what I was feeling.

I was going out to dinner in public with another man. That part didn't bother me. It was the fact that this was my first first-date since I had been in college, when I had first met and fallen in love with Danielle. Now Danielle was gone, and so was our baby girl, and I was standing here trying to pretend that I knew what I was doing.

I had no idea what I was doing, but I could fake it. And maybe I would think of this as a third date. That would be easier, after all.

The drive down to the city to a small hipster-like restaurant was easy. Getting out of the truck, though, wasn't.

Then I saw Archer slide out of his truck, run his hands nervously down his sides, and let out a breath. I wouldn't leave him to wait for long. When I saw a couple give him a look, one that implied need and desire, I got out that much quicker.

Because Archer was sexy as fuck, something I tried not to think about often, and yet, everyone that walked by him seemed to notice. But Archer didn't.

No, his ex had been an asshole, had hurt his self-esteem. So I was going to do my best not to be that person. I did not want to be like this Marc asshole. So I wouldn't. However, I would try not to be that Killian asshole I had been so good at.

We were off the main street where a lot of the college bars and bar crawls were for the universities in town, but there were still people milling about. Many of the older couples were probably associated with the university or Boulder city in general. Not as many college students. That made sense to me because when I had looked up this restaurant, the pricing wasn't exactly suited for college-age, nor was it as expensive and fancy as somewhere that Danielle's family would have gone.

Though they were up in Wyoming, they lived like they could walk down Fifth Avenue in New York City without a second glance or care in the world.

So, I had been to far nicer restaurants than these, and to mom-and-pop diners where I was afraid I would die from a heart attack. This, at least according to the website, seemed like an easy middle.

The fact that I had looked up the menu beforehand worried me. Why was I so nervous?

Then Archer smiled at me, and I let out a breath.

Oh, that was why.

"You made it."

I saw the relief in his eyes, and I could've kicked myself. "Of course I did. I wasn't going to stand you up."

Archer slid his hands into his back pockets, which wasn't an easy feat considering they were tight on his ass.

Hell, he looked delicious.

And now that I thought about it, we matched, him with a stone-blue shirt, and me with a stone-gray shirt.

Archer seemed to recognize it at the same time and smiled wide. A woman behind him nearly swooned, and I didn't blame her.

"It looks like we picked our uniform for the evening."

I rolled my eyes. "I wasn't sure what to wear."

"Good choice."

And then Archer reached for my arm, squeezed my elbow, and placed a kiss on the corner of my mouth.

I grinned, tilting my head as I studied him. "You're good at settling my nerves."

"I'm trying. I'm not the best at it. Because I'm nervous too, I don't date anymore."

"I'm going to go with what Penny said and name this our third date."

Archer's brows rose. "And why is that?"

"Because I haven't been on a first date since Danielle, and that made me a little ill."

Archer gave me a small nod in understanding. It didn't

say that he was upset by me mentioning my late wife. That wasn't who Archer was. He wanted to talk about my family. He wanted to know more. And I had to let him.

Then again, Danielle and my daughter weren't the only ghosts between us. A pretty large one had sent a wedding invitation to Archer. So I would have to live with that as well. But maybe that'd be okay. Maybe it would give me something to worry about that wasn't my own problem.

"I made a reservation, so we should be fine."

"Sounds good to me."

Archer led the way, and though we didn't hold hands, we did brush up against one another.

My heart stuttered slightly at that, trying to get used to this again.

"I feel like I don't know what I'm doing," I whispered as we walked up to the hostess stand.

"I'll help you figure it out."

The hostess led us to our table as everyone milled around, lost in their own dates and lives.

It was nice, the idea that we could be out in public, but not the center of attention. These days, when I was with others, I felt like they all knew my past and what issues I had.

I didn't like feeling the center of their attention, so this was better.

Not being stranded alone and wondering what people were thinking about when they saw me.

The hostess sat us down and handed us our menus, and I looked over at Archer.

"Nice place. I'm kind of glad that we aren't the only ones wearing jeans."

Archer smiled. "It's good food, not overly priced, but also not mom-and-pop diner priced."

"That's what I was just thinking." I let out a breath. "I did check out the menu online beforehand. I was nervous." There. I said it.

"Oh, good. Great. I did the same thing. I almost texted you to see what you were wearing, and then I realized that I was making too much of it."

"I assumed if we were going to a place where I had to wear a suit jacket, you would've let me know."

Archer just smiled. "Of course. I'm not going to lead you into a situation where both of us are out of our depth without advance notice."

"Good. I trust you."

I hadn't met to say that out loud, but it was the truth. And with the way that Archer's smile widened and his shoulders relaxed marginally, I realized it was the right thing to say.

I may have been a jerk to Archer at first to explain to him that he wasn't the only one hurting, but I hadn't paid attention enough to the fact that he was hurting. That fucker of an ex-husband had done a number on him. Well, I would have to be better than that. And remember that whatever Marc had done to Archer, Archer was coming out of it. And it was my job not to let him go back into it.

"Hello, I'm Trevor, and I'll be your server for the day." A

young man with bright purple hair, wearing a white collared shirt, black tie, and one of those long server's aprons came up to us.

He had an eyebrow ring and a nice smile. And with the way that he was looking at both Archer and me, it seemed that I wasn't the only one admiring the way Archer looked.

I didn't feel any jealousy, though, not with the way that Archer was smiling at me.

However, I did feel slightly old.

I couldn't help it. I had lived lifetimes, and sometimes it felt like those lifetimes were actual linear timeframes and not just experiences.

"Hi, Trevor, we're excited to be here."

I just shook my head at Archer as he tried to calm down my nerves.

I wasn't even sure he was aware he was doing it, but he was.

How had Marc not loved that? Or maybe he had taken advantage of it.

"Can I get you two started off with something to drink?"

"I know it's fall, but I heard they had a great rose here from one of my cousins."

"You have cousins that live here?" I asked, then held up my hand. "I'm sorry. You probably have cousins that live everywhere."

Archer laughed as Trevor gave us an odd look, probably trying to understand the joke.

"I'll have whatever you'd like. I trust you," I said.

Archer smiled even harder, and I felt like maybe I was doing something right.

"You have that bottle of rose that's pinot noir based?" Archer asked, scrunching his forehead as he tried to remember the name.

Trevor smiled. "I know exactly what you're talking about. And from the look of you, you must be Liam Montgomery's cousin."

"Yes, I am. I'm going to take that as a compliment, considering that Liam's a former model."

I snapped my fingers. "That's it."

"Oh good, I was hoping you would never know that. But then, I just out and blurted it."

Trevor laughed and said that he would come back with our drinks, as well as bread for the table, and I looked down at the menu, my shoulders shaking.

"Don't laugh."

"I'm just thinking. You could've been an underwear model like your cousin."

"I would like to think so, but then, everyone would've seen me in my underwear, not just you."

I raised a brow. "I don't actually remember seeing you in your underwear," I muttered, and Archer snorted, partially spilling his water.

"Then I guess next time we should take it slower. To make sure we take it all in."

"I was pretty sure you took it all in last time," I teased,

and Archer turned bright red, and I just shook my head, gulping my water. I couldn't believe I was joking like this.

Who the hell was I?

And why did Archer do this to me?

"What are you in the mood to eat?" I asked, and Archer raised a brow. I couldn't help but laugh. "So, this is what we're going to do, make sex jokes for the whole evening and call it a date?"

"Honestly, that sounds like a good time to me. However, we can talk about anything that you want. Or nothing. As for food, I was looking at the lavender and lemon roast chicken, with smashed potatoes, and broccolini."

"Lavender on chicken?" I asked and winced.

"My sisters made something like it, and I nearly inhaled all of it. What are you going to have?" Archer asked.

"I was thinking a steak. But now I feel like I'm boring."

Archer laughed, and then we sat back as the waiter handed us our drinks and our bread.

"Do you guys need a few minutes, or have you decided?" Trevor asked, looking at both of us.

"What are your specials?" Archer asked before I could say anything.

I gave him a grateful look as I continued to peruse the menu. For a guy who had looked it up before, I had no idea what I was doing. I was not good at this whole dating thing.

"We have a fresh butternut squash ravioli in a tomato reduction," he began, as he continued to talk I just sighed, trying to keep up.

Most days, I was a steak and baked potato man, or a chicken breast if I wanted to go healthy. I used to be better at this. But I guess being a hermit in my own home for so long meant that I didn't get out enough.

"And finally, we have a balsamic Ribeye that has the best marbling I've seen. It comes with smashed potatoes and grilled asparagus."

My stomach growled at that, and Archer beamed.

"What do you think? You want to go steak, but with a twist?"

"Would a balsamic glaze be good?" I asked, raising a brow. "Sorry," I said to Trevor. "I'm new at all this."

"No, it's fine. And it is quite wonderful. It doesn't take like you're licking vinegar or anything," he said with a laugh. "I can go through each layer of the flavors for you, or you can just trust me."

I looked at Archer, who just shrugged. "Trust him. And if you don't like it, we'll get you something else."

"I'm not going to waste a steak. Let's do this."

"That sounds great. What about appetizers?"

"There's a goat cheese and beet salad that looks amazing," Archer began, and I shook my head. "Whatever you want. I am clearly the one that's behind on all this."

"I have just the thing for both of you," Trevor said as he took our menus and left, leaving me dumbfounded.

"Is he going to order us an appetizer?"

"Who knows. But I think you made an impression."

That made me laugh. "No, Archer, you're the one that made an impression."

"Or maybe it's the both of us," Archer said as he wiggled his brows.

"You know, I don't think I could ever share. I'm not a poly type of guy."

"Honestly, same. Two of my cousins are in poly relationships and they make it work, but it's not for me."

My brows rose. "Really? That's pretty cool."

"Very much so. They're all parents now, or at least becoming parents, so they have dealt with the legality of being in a poly relationship, with powers of attorney and everything. So I guess if any of my siblings decided to add a third to their pairings, they would have an outline."

"They should write a book."

"Maybe. Or maybe it can just go down into the Montgomery family bible."

"I'm a little worried to think of what that bible would contain."

Trevor came back, with the beet salad in one hand and some form of mushroom thing in the other.

"These are our stuffed mushrooms with cheese. Since you ordered goat cheese, I assumed you'd be okay with that type of dairy."

"That looks amazing," I said as I looked down at it. "Thank you."

"It's on us."

Archer raised a brow. "You don't have to do that, Trevor."

"No, we do. The owners like Liam and your sister Paige."

I gave Archer a look as he winced.

"Let me guess. They know her ex?" Archer asked, his voice slightly cold.

Trevor nodded. "I remember him too. Great chef, but we loved Paige more. So, you get mushroom caps on us."

"Thank you," Archer said as he looked down at the food, and I met his gaze as Trevor walked away.

"Do I want to know?"

"I will tell you the whole sordid story of how finding restaurants in this state is getting a little challenging."

I took a bite of the mushrooms and nearly moaned in glee. As the two of us ate, I learned more about being a Montgomery.

And I felt like everything just clicked, like I wasn't making mistake after mistake.

I just shook my head and leaned into the conversation, learning more and actually answering questions when Archer had them.

This felt natural, as if we had done this a thousand times. It should worry me, and maybe it did, but not enough.

The steak melted in my mouth, the balsamic glaze was perfection, and the lavender chicken held up to the hype as well.

By the time we were done, Archer followed me back to

my house, and though I wasn't sure what would happen next, I didn't want the evening to end, and clearly Archer didn't either.

When we pulled up to the place, I cursed loudly and stepped out of the car, turning off the engine.

"What the fuck?" I growled.

Paint smears of the gray and stone colors that I had picked for the outside were all over the rocks, windows, and boards that had covered where the broken glass had been before.

"Killian. This is bad."

"Could it be kids? But kids aren't that vicious. Not really."

"I don't know. But you're going to call the cops, right?"

The mood completely deflated after our date. I nodded and picked up my phone.

"You can head home if you want to. I'm afraid it's going to be a long night."

Archer stepped towards me, frowned, then kissed me square on the lips. "If you think you are doing this alone, you have another think coming."

"I don't know what to do now," I whispered, hope and tension sliding through me.

"Well, you're not alone. Cora is with Penny?"

Alarm shot through me and I nodded. "Can you call her? Check on them. Just in case."

Archer picked up his phone and dialed Penny, as I called the cops.

I looked at the man with whom I'd had one of the most pleasant evenings I'd had in a while and wondered what I had done to deserve him. I wasn't sure, but I'd have to keep it up.

I also had to figure out who the fuck was hurting this property and why they kept coming back.

Chapter Fourteen

Archer

Three weeks. Three weeks of work, sweat, meetings, and Killian. Three weeks of figuring out exactly who we could be together as we took the next steps into whatever the hell we were.

I still couldn't quite believe it had *only* been three weeks and had already been three weeks since our first date.

"I'm a little worried," Killian said as he walked into his bedroom, buttoning up his shirt.

I tried not to be sad that he was closing off his muscles to me, but I would still be able to see them when he moved, so that was something.

"Eyes up here, Montgomery."

I guiltily raised my eyes from his now-clothed chest and grinned up at him.

"I can't help it. You're pretty."

He grunted as he shook his head, his blond hair falling over his forehead.

"What are you worried about?"

"What do you think I'm worried about?"

I winced. "The fact that the cops haven't figured out who did this to your house?"

Killian looked up and blinked at me. "Well, yes, but I wasn't thinking about that. I was thinking about the fact that I'm going to a family dinner."

"Oh. So, I probably shouldn't have brought up the whole vandalism thing."

I winced and lowered my head, feeling like an idiot. Of course, Killian hadn't wanted the reminder that somebody kept trying to harm his property. A property that had meant so much to him because he was building it for his wife and daughter. I knew the symbolism behind the place and why he was working hard, not sleeping, and continuing to put blood, sweat, and tears into it.

I hurt because he was hurting, and was angry that someone was trying to damage the place. I understood why Killian still needed to build this place. Just because we were together now didn't mean he had to drop everything from his past and ignore it.

"I'm sorry. I didn't mean to bring that up."

Killian cursed under his breath. "Don't apologize to me.

Yes, I'm still worried about that. But you don't have to ball yourself up into the corner and pretend that what happened didn't happen. You don't have to hide from me or feel bad about bringing something up. I'm not fucking Marc."

I looked up at him then, and I could feel the blood drain from my face.

"Are you serious right now? That's what you're bringing up? 'I'm not Marc.'"

"Fuck. That's not what I meant."

"What did you mean? Because you're right, I wasn't good about standing up to Marc. Even if he never hit me, he still made me feel like shit. I don't want to feel like shit here."

"And yet you were making yourself feel like shit just now because you thought you said something to hurt me. You didn't."

"Then why are we fighting?" I asked, my voice rising.

"Because I don't like it when you're hard on yourself. Because when you are, it just reminds me that I can't hurt that man, and then I feel like you're comparing me to him."

"That's not what I'm doing, and you know it."

"I really don't, Archer. I'm still getting used to this whole thing."

"Fine. Me too."

"Okay. Everything's okay."

"I don't want to fuck this up. And I know you're not Marc."

"I'll try not to bring him up. That was wrong of me."

"It really was. I don't think you're Marc. And maybe

sometimes I'll react like you are because it's habit, but I'm getting better."

Killian was there then, cupping my face. I wanted to lean into him, but I was so afraid, because he was right. Marc had done this. Lashed out at me, made me feel small, and then had warmed to me, making me feel better.

Killian wasn't Marc, and I needed to be better than this.

"I am worried about the vandalism. But it's been three weeks since anything else happened, so maybe it was just kids or passersby. The authorities don't have anything, we're being safe, and Cora is never alone at the house." Something dark flashed over his eyes before he continued. "Penny's keeping an eye out, and so are all the other neighbors."

"The neighbors sure do like you. They're all rallying around you."

He shrugged. This time it was him blushing.

"The neighbors are nice. Don't know what they see in me, but whatever."

"I could tell you what they see in you, but I don't know if you'd believe me."

"Maybe."

Killian leaned forward and kissed me soundly on the mouth before he moved back to go put on his watch. "All I'm saying, though, is that yes, I am a little nervous about meeting your family in full and not just talking to someone on the phone for work things. However, you don't need to cower in on yourself like you thought you had to do with Marc if you're afraid of upsetting me. I'm not him."

"I know that." I let out a breath. "I know that. But you also don't have to bring him up like that."

"Maybe. Maybe we both need to be better. I'm not good at this whole thing."

"Neither am I, but we can maybe be poor at it together?" I asked, my voice going a little high-pitched.

"If that's what we need to do," he teased.

"Are you sure this is right? That I should be going to this? Because the last time I met with my significant other's family, they shouted at me, pushed me away, and told me that I was a horrible person because their daughter and granddaughter were dead, and I was still alive."

I moved to him then and held him close. "We don't have to do this tonight. If this is too quick for you, we don't have to go."

He let out a shuddering breath as I wrapped my arms around him, my chest pressing to his back.

"I'm not good at this whole thing. I never fit in with Danielle's parents."

"The good thing about the Montgomerys is everyone fits in with us. We're a handy bunch."

"Maybe, or maybe I'll just sit in the corner and watch you guys like I'm watching the Discovery network."

"That could work too," I teased. "We are interesting."

"You are. That's why I like spending time with you."

I blinked. "Really?" I asked, blushing.

"Of course, really. It's why I'm here, after all. And why

you're here. You brought me out of my shell just a bit, Archer."

I looked over his shoulder into the mirror, our gazes meeting. "Are you sure?" I asked softly.

"Yes, I'm sure. I wasn't good with Danielle's family, but our family was strong. The one that we made with the four of us, including Cora," he said as the Lab leaned against us. "And I know I'm going with you tonight because your family wants to meet me because, apparently, I was such an asshole to you before that they're worried."

"That's not the case," I said, hoping I wasn't lying.

"It seems like a little bit of a case," he said after a moment. "I know that I'm not easy. That I'm not ready for anything beyond what we have now."

I smiled softly. "I'm not either. That's why we're taking it slow. However, you are meeting my entire family. At least, my entire immediate family."

"I'm not going to the whole reunion, am I?" he asked, his eyes wide. "I mean, I like you, Archer. A lot. But I don't think I'm ready for nine hundred Montgomerys."

That made me laugh. "I don't think we're that many. At least, I hope there aren't that many. Mom and I are still working on the plans for the reunion, and I don't have that many invites out."

"You still have enough time for her, if you're spending a lot of your evenings with me?"

"You're spending just as many evenings with me," I

added. "But I'm trying. And my mom likes my help. This reunion is going to be fucking amazing."

"That's good. And I still don't know if I'm ready for that."

"Nobody's ready for that. I'm not going to force you to go." However, I did feel a little odd about that, actually. But I had to remind myself it'd only been three weeks since our date, six weeks or so since we had met. A huge family reunion was probably a little too much too soon. Even for me, the guy who liked happily ever afters as quickly as possible. But I had tried that with Marc and it hadn't turned out too well, so maybe going as slow as possible this time was good. Of course, Killian and I were already sleeping together, and I was taking him to a family dinner, but that was my version of slow.

"Okay, let's go. We're dropping of Cora at Penny's, and then we're heading back down to Fort Collins."

"The drive is a lot, isn't it?" I asked, trying to be casual.

There was nothing casual about what I was saying, though, and Killian could hear it in my voice.

"It is a bit of a drive. But you're here for the house often enough."

"I am," I said after a moment.

"What's wrong?"

"Nothing," I lied. I needed to be better than that, to not lie, but I also needed a moment to think, because frankly, I was worried. Worried because I was starting to fall for him.

And it was far too soon. And the last time I had fallen too soon, I had broken.

I didn't want to break again.

"Let's get there," I said and smiled, telling myself that I was doing much better than I had in the past. I was getting to be happy. Something I hadn't thought I could do before. Yes, I had been finding my happiness along the way on my own, with my work, with this project that was finally coming along for Robert and Evelyn's home, the property next to Killian's. But now I was finding out who I was with someone. Someone that made me happy. Someone who didn't treat me like I needed to change.

I swallowed hard and followed Killian to my car after dropping off Cora with Penny. The woman had winked at me, smiled, and then kissed me on the cheek before pushing me out of the house. We were taking my car down to my family's house because we planned to spend the night in my apartment.

The apartment that felt a little too small for the two of us, but there was not much I could do about that now. I needed to figure out what I wanted to do in the next few months because my lease would be up. Did I want to build a new house? Find one that a Montgomery already built? Or do the unthinkable and buy the house of my heart?

Tonight was not about those thoughts though. Tonight was about a family dinner.

The drive was quiet, the two of us enjoying a podcast that was about one of our favorite books, and we finally pulled up to Annabelle's house, the last ones to arrive, if how many cars were out front was any indication.

"There sure are a lot of you," Killian mumbled, running his hands up and down his thighs.

I reached out and gripped his hand, consoling him. "We can walk away right now. If this is too much, we do not have to be here."

"No, it's fine. I'm okay." He looked at me, then smiled. It was like a kick in the gut, and I let out a breath.

"If you're sure?"

"I'm sure. I'm okay. I'm just getting used to this. This is a new experience. And I told myself I needed to try those."

"Okay. Just be warned. The Montgomerys are loud, and we love cheese."

"That's why I brought the gifts." He pulled out the two bags and I smiled, knowing exactly what was in each, since I helped him pick them out.

"Okay. Just be warned, we like hugs."

"Oh," he said, blanching.

"But they won't hug you right away. They'll give you space."

"How much do they know about me?" he asked suddenly, his body going still.

"Not everything. That wasn't my story to tell."

His shoulders relaxed, and I was doubly grateful that I hadn't betrayed his trust by telling them anything more than I already had.

We got out of the car and made our way up front, where Annabelle opened the door quickly and rushed out.

"It's my favorite brother," Annabelle exclaimed as both Benjamin and Beckett cursed from behind her inside the house.

"My favorite twin," I added as I swung Annabelle into my arms and twirled her.

"So happy to see you. It feels like it's been ages."

"It was yesterday," I corrected. "At the office."

"Oh, stop. Just let me have this." She kissed me on the cheek. I set her down and she turned to Killian. "You must be Killian. It's wonderful to meet you." She held out her hand as I wrapped my arm around her shoulders, and Killian took it graciously.

"It's lovely to meet you, Annabelle. The twin that I've been hearing so much about."

"Only good things, I hope." She beamed, and I could tell it wasn't forced. She was truly happy for me. I tried not to stress out at that. "Come on in. We're a loud and rambunctious group. But we don't bite. That, I can promise you."

"I don't know if I can promise that," I mumbled, and Killian choked into his fist as we walked inside.

Everybody was standing around, joking, and they waved at Leif, who stood next to Lee and Paige, blending into the family as if he'd been here all along.

"Okay, so here's everybody," I said, clearing my throat. "Everybody, this is Killian."

"Hi Killian," everybody said at the same time, as if they were in a classroom meeting the new teacher.

I cringed. "You guys, be good."

"Of course, we'll be good," Paige said as she bounced forward. "It's so nice to meet you, Killian." She held out her hand too, and Killian gave me a look.

"I told you, we're huggers, but we give space first."

"But not for long," Lee warned. "They come at you quickly after you get used to them."

"We do lull you into a false sense of security," Leif added.

"So I've been warned," Killian said as he shook Paige's hand.

"Well, let me see him," Mom said as she came forward, a smile on her face.

I held back a groan. "Mom."

"Don't 'Mom' me. I'm having a good day, and you can't stop me," she winked and held out her hands to Killian. "I will hug you next time, I'm just warning you. Unless you tell me you don't like hugs, and then I will respect your wishes."

"I think I can start getting used to hugs. Slowly," Killian warned as he held out one of the bags. "For you."

"For me?"

"And this is for you," he said as he held it up to Annabelle. Annabelle clapped her hands and held the bag close. "I wasn't sure what you both liked, so I figured one for the house and one for the matriarch. If I made a complete mistake, please let me know. I'm rusty at this."

"We'll just have to make sure you come over to our houses next," Paige said as she looked at Eliza.

"Yes. We like gifts, but this way, you don't have to go all out each time."

As both Annabelle and mom opened their gifts, they laughed, looking at the cheese baskets that he had given each of them.

"I figured you could share it with everyone."

"You brought in cheese. He is the one," Paige joked, and I scowled at her, grateful that Killian was talking to both Beckett and Benjamin as they quietly grilled him. That meant Killian hadn't heard that, and as Paige blushed and shook her head, I narrowed my eyes.

Be better, I mouthed at her, and she just shrugged before we all went back to the dining room table, and Mom and Annabelle began setting out the cheeses.

"This will be perfect for our appetizers."

"You don't need to eat it right now," Killian hedged.

"Oh, we will. Cheese doesn't last long in his family," my twin teased.

As people started to dive into the goat and Havarti cheeses that Killian brought, the man I was falling for laughed. "I can see that."

Leif came up to us and grinned. "I didn't get to meet you yet. Hi, I'm Leif."

"Are you another Montgomery?" Killian asked, and I knew he was doing the family tree in his head. "I'm sorry. I don't remember how you're related."

Leif just laughed. "I'm their cousin's kid. So, I guess a second cousin, but sometimes I call them uncles."

"You look almost Archer's age," Killian said. "Sorry. I think I'm losing my mind trying to keep up."

"I'm not that much younger. There's a lot of Montgomerys, and we span all ages. Some of my cousins and even my siblings are younger than some of Archer's nieces and nephews. You get used to it."

"Apparently, I'm going to have to," Killian said, and right then and there, I knew I was in trouble.

Because I was trying not to think serious. I was trying not to go beyond the now, just go into the healing of a new relationship.

But with the way that Killian was trying so hard for my family?

I was in trouble.

I was falling in love with Killian Hart.

Chapter Fifteen

Killian

It had been a few weeks since the last issue on the property. My head ached, but not about that. It was about the guilt that had slowly wrapped itself around me.

Because, while the authorities couldn't figure out what was going on with the vandalism on my place, I had to focus on something else. Namely, wondering if I was doing the right thing.

I knelt down in the smooth grass, grateful to the caretakers for dealing with any weeds. Wildflowers bloomed over the mounds in front of me, and I slid my hands over them, careful not to pluck them, to let them live free and wild.

"Danielle, Cassidy. I know it's been a few weeks since

I've been here, but I think about you every day. I know you know that. I know you can hear it in my voice, and I feel you with me as I work around the house that should have been ours." I looked at Danielle's gravestone, then turned to my daughter's. It was smaller, the date so short that I could barely hold in the rage.

Six years on this earth.

It wasn't fair that Cassidy was gone, that the cold and ice had taken her from me before she had a chance to live. She hadn't learned who she was, hadn't found her happiness. I hoped that whatever I had done for her had given her some joy. That Cora and her little puppy barks had given her a life that was worth living.

But fate had decided to end my daughter's life far too soon, and the guilt that riddled me for being the one left behind wasn't going to go away.

Sometimes I could breathe through the ebb and flow of day-to-day monotony, and sometimes I could barely stand up straight.

I looked at Danielle's stone and swallowed hard. "Hey, baby. I'm trying. You always told me to try, to smile more, to be in the moment. I remember that. Sometimes I was so focused on work and the projects that I wasn't the man you needed me to be. But I'm trying. I always will be. Archer's changing things. It feels weird to say his name around you, but you know him. You see him. I feel you around when he's there. I don't know if I'm supposed to be feeling this way. Or if I'm making a mistake. I just hope that I'm not moving too quickly." The wind slid through the long grass around the cemetery and I looked up at the sky, closing my eyes as I tried to suck in deep breaths.

"I miss you."

I lowered my head, opened my eyes, and stared at the stones that marked a place of life and death. Danielle and Cassidy were no longer here. I knew that. Intellectually and spiritually, I knew that. They were gone, and any presence that I felt around me were their memories. I didn't want them to still be here. I wanted them to be free. To be on that other plane of existence and to be doing what they needed to in order to find peace.

I was just the one left behind. And it had taken me three years to come to terms with the fact that maybe being left behind didn't mean fading along the way.

It had taken seeing Archer. It had taken calling my sister back. It had taken Cora pushing me. It had taken Penny smiling at me and guiding me on a path I wasn't ready for.

It had taken all of them, and now it would have to be up to me.

"I love you both. I will until the end of my days. I'm not okay. But I'm finding my way. I think you both would like Archer." I looked at Cassidy's grave and smiled softly. "He would have loved you. You would have danced and played on the playground. He can do a back handspring. He's pretty spry. I never could do that. But you were learning your walkover, and he could have helped you. Of course, in another lifetime, we never would have met, but I like to think that you would have loved him, Cassidy." I let out a shaky breath and wiped the tears from my face.

"I think you would have loved him, too, Danielle." I was falling in love with him. But I didn't say that out loud. I couldn't. Not yet. Nobody was ready for that. "He's trying so hard to find out who he is. He works longer hours than I do sometimes. I think he doesn't even realize that he's trying to find his place within his family even though they want him to just be who he is. Nobody's pushing him in a corner; he's doing it to himself. He could be so many things, and they're allowing it because they love him. I just hope he realizes it."

I let out a breath. "Somebody's hurting the house that I wanted to build for us. I don't know who it is or what they want, but they're hurting it. And I feel like they're hurting us in the process. I don't know what to do about it, other than try to catch them. But they evaded the security camera I put up, so I don't know if it's the same person or if we just have a string of bad luck. I want to protect the home that I was building for you both. Even though neither of you will be there."

I let out a shaky breath. "I don't know what I'm supposed to do now. But I'm trying." A warm breeze brushed my face, as if someone was cupping my cheek, and I swallowed hard. "I'm trying for you. And for Cassidy. And Cora. And Ann. And Penny. And Archer." I sucked in a breath. "And for me. I'm trying. I promise."

I stayed for a few more minutes before I stood up and

made my way to my truck. Another truck pulled in behind me, and Branson got out.

My former father-in-law glared at me from underneath the rim of his cowboy hat, the black material dull in the bright lights.

"You got a lot of nerve showing up here," Branson snarled.

"Have a good day, Branson."

"Can't do that now, can I?" Branson snapped before shouldering past me. "You best keep away. We don't want your kind here."

I barely held back the roll of my eyes at Branson's words. My father-in-law was a fucking asshole and always had been. We were on public property. This wasn't their land. I had let my girls be buried in Wyoming near her family, but they were my family too. So I hadn't allowed them to be buried on the family property. Danielle hadn't wanted that, so I had respected her wishes. And that meant I could visit my wife and daughter. Because Branson would never allow that if they were buried on family land.

Her family had never liked me, but it had gotten worse, because they blamed me for her death.

In the end, though, nothing they could do could hurt me worse than I already was. Because I still blamed myself every day for what happened. Because I lived, and they didn't.

I made my way back down to Boulder, pissed off at

myself. Because this feeling was just reminding me what I wasn't ready for. To fucking live.

I pulled into the driveway and didn't see Archer's truck, but I did see his team. They must be working on the upgrades to the new house today, and Archer was probably on a job down in Fort Collins, where he lived and needed to be.

Not with me.

Cora bounced towards me as I got out of the truck, and I knelt down and gave her love before I stood up.

I wanted to hit something with a hammer. I just needed to work, and since it didn't look like there had been any more vandalism since the paint, I wanted to count that as a win. Because I needed a win.

"You look like you're having one of those days," Penny said as she walked towards me, a plate of sugar cookies in her hand.

"Hi, Penny. Thanks for taking care of Cora. She loves the drive, but there wasn't really a good place to keep her where I was."

"I understand. Cora gets to speak to her ladies every time she smiles in her sleep."

I frowned. "Penny."

"Eat a cookie and shut the fuck up."

My brows rose, and I reached for a cookie, freezing. "There's nothing especially green in this, is there?"

"These are not weed sugar cookies. I would never lace something without telling you. I'm not a monster."

"Okay."

"But there is a sugar substitute in this. Monkfruit."

I froze. "What?"

"You've had it before and didn't know it. You love it."

"That just completely negates what you just said."

"I'm not putting drugs in your cookies. I'm putting sugar substitutes just to see if you can taste the difference. You couldn't, so count that as a win. Eat."

I took a cookie, bit into the softness of it, and nearly moaned.

"This is amazing."

"You don't have to growl and sound so surly about it."

"I feel like I do."

"Do you want to talk about it?"

I shook my head. "Not in the least."

"Good, because you're going to talk about it."

"Then why did you fucking ask?"

"Because I fucking can. If you're going to curse, so am I, dickhead."

I looked at Penny then, threw my head back, and laughed. "You annoy me so fucking much."

"Of course I do. It's why you love me. Now, tell me what hurts."

I looked at her then and then took another cookie. "Everything hurts. You know that."

"Okay. Everything hurts. Talk to me, Killian. That's what I'm here for."

"You're here for more than that, Penny."

Her eyes widened fractionally, and that's when I realized I had been an asshole to more than just Archer.

"I'm sorry, Penny. I do appreciate you."

"I know. I'm good at forcing myself into your life. But I got Cora out of the deal, so in all reality, that's all that matters."

She leaned down and pressed herself against the Lab as Cora gave her best doggie smile.

"I don't know what we would have done without you."

"Cora would make sure you find your way."

"Maybe."

"You're allowed to live, Killian. You've been doing so these past few weeks. The difference has been remarkable."

"Why do I feel like I'm making a mistake?"

"Because you're scared. And you're allowed to be scared. But you don't have to be. That's the difference."

I swallowed hard, then reached for another cookie.

"Last one, boy. You don't want to get sick."

"I always knew I could count on you to take care of me."

"Always. Now, I do believe somebody's coming up here to say hello, and you should let yourself be."

I turned as Archer came forward, takeout boxes in his hand.

"Well, I see I may have been too late with the food. Are those sugar cookies?" Archer asked, his eyes bright.

"They are, young man, these are for both of you. Now I'm going to go take Cora on a walk."

At the W-word, Cora started to bounce.

"You don't have to do that, Penny."

"Yes, I do. I want the company. Now, go make some company of your own." She shoved the plate of cookies at me, and I shook my head and looked over at Archer.

"I like that she takes care of you. It's sweet." Archer leaned forward, kissed me softly on the lips, and I sighed.

"What's wrong?" he whispered.

"I went up to Wyoming today," I blurted, not realizing I was going to say the words.

Archer's eyes widened, and then he hugged me tight, the food in between us. "Are you okay? No, that's not a good question even to ask. Do you want to talk about anything? Or do you want to just eat?"

"It depends on what you brought to eat," I teased, and Archer's shoulders relaxed.

"Well, if you're going to joke around, I'm going to count that as progress."

I met his gaze and then leaned forward and kissed him softly on the mouth. "Progress," I whispered against his lips.

"As for food," he said as we walked into the house, "I brought with me Greek food from my favorite place in Fort Collins."

I raised my brows. "And it's still warm?"

"I had it in an insulated pouch, thank you very much. We have Greek potatoes, gyros, chicken kebab, basmati rice, and some marinated mushrooms."

"I think my mouth is watering."

Archer beamed. "I also got baklava, but I think these

sugar cookies are going to beat it."

"I'm good for anything, I'm starving." I put my hand over my stomach. "I didn't eat breakfast or lunch."

"Killian, that's not you taking care of yourself." Archer narrowed his eyes.

I shrugged. "Didn't feel like eating."

"Do you want to talk about it at all?" Archer asked as he set out our food.

I let out a breath, trying to do what Danielle and Cassidy would want me to do. "I went up there to talk. I do that sometimes. It wasn't for any one thing." I sighed as I reached for a potato. Archer slapped my hand and handed me a fork, and I grinned before I bit into the lemony goodness. "My God."

"Right?" Archer teased as he took the fork from me and ate the rest of the potato.

I cleared my throat. "I brought you up when I was talking to them." Archer choked, and I patted his back. "Sorry."

"No, it's fine. I just, I don't know what to say about it." He met my gaze, and I sucked in a breath, trying to calm my own feelings, which were currently going in a thousand different directions.

"I just told them a bit about you, but I assumed they already knew about you."

"That's nice. That they would know. I hope they do. I don't have an experience like that, but I want you to know I'll do whatever you need."

"Because you're a good man."

And I'm falling in love with you.

Again, I didn't say those words out loud.

Archer smiled sappily. "You do make my heart go boom. We're going to call that a win." He fluttered his eyelashes, and I groaned before I leaned forward and took his lips with mine.

This time it wasn't soft or sweet. It was just a little bit harder.

"What is it about you and me and kitchens?"

"What do you say we reheat this food later, your insulated pack be damned?" I muttered against his lips, and I felt more than saw Archer swallow hard.

"I think I would like to see your bedroom right now." We put the food away, and then we were kissing softly, leading each other back to the bedroom.

Archer's hand slid up my chest as he stripped off my shirt, and I groaned at the feel of his callused palms over my flesh.

I shucked off his shirt, and then we were doing the same to each other's pants, both of us taking our time.

It was nice, it was hot, but it wasn't frantic. It was just the two of us learning each other again, getting to know the feel of one another.

We lay on the bed, facing each other as we kissed, our hands sliding over one another. My hand brushed his backside, and he thrust into me, our dicks sliding against one another, and when Archer did the same to me, spreading me slightly, I groaned, kissing him.

"This is nice," I whispered.

"The best appetizer ever."

And then I was pinning Archer to the bed, kissing him hard on the mouth as I straddled him. I couldn't help it.

He let out a raspy breath as I shimmied down his body, taking his dick in my hand as I knelt between his legs.

"That's a sight that I love."

"I hope so, because I'm damn sure enjoying it." And then I took his cock into my mouth, cupping his balls as I did so. I went slow, tasting him, learning the feel of him in my mouth, like it was our first time and not one of many.

Archer slid his hands through my hair, and both of us groaned as I knelt before him, taking more and more of him in.

I relaxed my jaw and swallowed more, the tip of his dick brushing the back of my throat and deeper.

"Holy hell," Archer grunted as I made a sucking noise against him.

He was big, slightly thicker than me, though not as long.

The fact that we had literally compared each other's dicks one day in the shower made me smile along his length. Because we had laughed, then each of us had taken turns figuring out exactly how we measured up, both realizing that we were what the other person needed right then and there.

Perhaps he could be what I needed for more.

I wasn't ready for that, and I pushed those thoughts out of my head.

Instead, I continued to bob my head up and down before Archer let out a sharp groan and tugged at my hair.

"I'm going to come."

I didn't pull back. Instead, I swallowed every inch of him as he came, hot and salty down my throat as he rasped my name, his body shaking.

"Okay, I wasn't expecting that," Archer said, his body slick with sweat as he took in deep gulps of air.

And then I was moving across him, kissing him hard on the mouth, before rolling him on his belly.

I opened the bedside table, pulled out lube and a condom as Archer dreamily looked up at me. "Ass up in the air, Archer. I want to see what I'm going to play with."

"Whatever you say, sir," he mock-laughed.

"You know, I kind of like it when you call me sir."

Archer's brows raised even as his eyes went wild. "If those are the games you want to play, we're going to have to have an entirely different conversation."

I rolled my eyes. I couldn't believe I was smiling and laughing right then. After the morning that I had, here I was with another man, but I didn't feel ashamed. It was just the two of us, enjoying one another.

I worked Archer slowly, preparing him for me, then I slid the condom over my length and slowly breached his entrance. My cock was so damn hard, stretching him, even though I'd already used two fingers to ready him.

I went slow because, no matter what, I would not hurt Archer.

That was my goal in life, in my existence. I could not hurt him.

And when he pushed back, so I was fully seated in him, I let out a raspy breath.

"You're so tight."

"Sweetest fucking things," Archer whispered.

And then I was moving, and so was he. I pulled him up, so his back was to my chest, and I wrapped my hand around his newly hard cock.

I thrust in and out of him slowly, not going too hard, just hard enough for both of us to feel it.

Archer put his arm over his head, wrapped his palm around the back of my neck, and we turned our heads slightly to kiss, our mouths meeting at a frantic pace.

I kept thrusting as Archer moved back into me, and then I was coming, and Archer was coming, having come so quickly after his first that I couldn't help but grin.

And I couldn't breathe in this moment, knowing that he was mine.

As we lay there, knowing that our dinner was getting cold, the two of us were sweat-slicked and only semi-sated, I was afraid of what was going to happen next.

Because this was too happy. Too good.

And I didn't get good things. Not anymore.

The room grew chilled, but Archer didn't notice, and I prayed he wouldn't.

For this moment, I just had to hope he couldn't.

Chapter Sixteen

Archer

I laid kisses along Killian's back and he arched into me, the two of us slowly waking up for the day.

I reached around, gripped him, and he groaned, his whole body shaking underneath me.

"Archer. Good morning."

I smiled lazily against his back.

"I think it's the best morning we could have," I whispered.

"We have to hurry," he mumbled.

"Oh yeah?" I asked, as I began to ready him.

"Yes. You have to head to Fort Collins, and I have a meeting with the window people."

"So domestic," I teased, and then could have rightly kicked myself. I didn't want to bring us out of the moment even thinking about what the future could be.

I didn't want to scare him away.

I continued to work him, as we leaned into one another, our lips meeting, our breaths coming in pants.

When I reached around and gripped him again, and slid my hand over his length, he groaned, before pressing into me.

"Archer. Go already."

I smiled and then slowly eased in and out of him, breeching his entrance as we both moaned. I paused, taking a deep breath, and then I continued to move, inch by achingly slow inch, until I was firmly seated. He was so tight around me, I could barely catch my breath. Killian's arms shook as he knelt in front of me.

This wasn't our first time in this position, as we enjoyed taking each other in different ways, but this felt different. As if this was a normal morning routine.

"Archer."

"I've got you," I whispered, and then I moved.

Slowly, painstakingly slow.

I pulled out, and then pressed back in, both of us letting out a moan as he tightened around me.

I slid my arm around him, working him as we both shook.

I could barely hold on, barely breathe, but I needed to focus.

This was Killian. The man I was falling for. The man I was doing my best not to fall for too quickly. Because I didn't want to worry him. Didn't want to make him think that he needed to fall for me.

So I just kept moving, ignoring the pressures, and just focused on him.

And when he groaned, the guttural growl as my name slid over his lips, I pushed into him.

"Killian," I growled out.

"Archer."

And then he spent on the sheets, coming in my hand, as I filled the condom, arching my back, spurting hot seed.

We both fell in a tangle of limbs, and I gently, oh so gently, pulled out of him.

"My god," he whispered.

"We're getting pretty good at that."

I leaned down and kissed his shoulder.

"You could say that."

I looked at him then, and knew I was in love. Right then and there.

It was a different kind of love than I had before, but I was in love.

But I couldn't say it yet. It was too early. Not with what he had gone through. But maybe I could show him.

I swallowed hard, then took his lips.

"I need to clean you up."

"And probably the sheets. And I hear whining at the door."

"I'm kind of sorry I closed the door on her, I like waking up with Cora cuddled on us."

"But she doesn't need to see this. We don't want to scare her."

"No, we don't."

"Let's clean up quickly, be right back."

I slid off the bed, took care of the condom, grabbed a washcloth, and went back to the bed. I gently cleaned up Killian as we kissed, and then I was stripping off the sheets as Killian pulled on pants and went to go walk Cora.

Again, so domestic, but it felt right.

My phone buzzed and I looked down on it.

Mom: Will I see you today soon? Do you want breakfast? Or will the drive be too much?

I smiled and picked up the phone and texted as I walked towards the small laundry that Killian had recently put in.

Me: I'll be there before lunch. I'll probably pick up something to eat here. It's a bit of a drive.

That familiar pang at the idea that it was a long drive for me to get back to my home worried me. There was a reason that I was worried. Because Killian lived way the fuck out here, and the home I was working on might be close to him, but it wasn't the home I lived in. Nor it was where all my family was.

Mom: Okay. I'll do a nice lunch spread. I can't wait to see you. And talk reunion!

She put a few smiley emojis, and I grinned.

Mom was so excited about this reunion. It wasn't like we

didn't see all of the family often, but having them all in one place at one time was a big deal. And the fact that this was the first time she was doing this on her own, the Fort Collins branch representing, meant the world to her.

I wasn't going to let her down.

I finished cleaning up as Killian came back in and smiled.

I swallowed hard at the sight of him in nothing but pajama bottoms, and shook my head as Cora bounded in and went to her haunches in front of me.

I knelt in front of her and rubbed her down.

"Who's a good girl?"

"She's the best," Killian said as he shook his head and began to make coffee.

"I need to shower and head out. I hope that's okay?"

"The window guys will be here in an hour, so how about I hook us up with some toast and bacon. Eggs?"

"It sounds great." I smiled at him, and he smiled right back, his eyes full of an emotion I couldn't read.

Would I be so lucky that he could love me back? I wasn't sure, but this felt good.

He had already braved a Montgomery family dinner. If he could do that, I figured perhaps he could do anything.

"Killian, I know this is odd to ask, but did you want to come to the reunion with me?" I blurted without thinking.

I froze, afraid I had said too much. Because that was a big deal. Attending a family reunion when you weren't family? That was like laying claim in front of everyone else.

But Killian didn't stiffen or look worried. Instead, he

raised a brow at me. "Your mom already invited me, but thanks. I guess I can go as your date, too."

I laughed, relief pouring over me.

"Good. When did she invite you?"

"She texted."

I groaned. "Mom is texting you?"

"Not often. Just to ask about the reunion. We exchanged phone numbers because she was worried about you being out here all alone, even though you are with your team more often than not."

"Well, that's not embarrassing at all."

Killian shook his head as he walked towards me, the bacon set on the cookie sheet to go into the oven. He cupped my face as Cora stood between us and gently kissed me. "Don't be embarrassed. It's good that people love you. That they care about you. Okay? I don't mind. If I did mind, I'd act growly. And I'm not growly. At least right now."

Warmth infused me, and I swallowed hard.

"Okay."

Then he kissed me softly, patted me on the butt, and I went to go take a shower, leaving him to make our breakfast, that new sense of domesticity sliding between us.

The drive back to Fort Collins took forever thanks to an accident on the highway, but I pulled into my parents' house's driveway on time. I had wanted to be earlier than this, but I couldn't change that.

Mom opened the door before I had even had a chance to knock and threw her arms open.

"It feels like I haven't seen you in forever." She held me close and I kissed the top of her head.

"Well, I like this welcome. And I just saw you like four days ago."

"But not here. I don't know, all my babies are putting down roots everywhere else, and I'm just feeling old."

I blinked. "Mom. Where's this coming from?"

She shook her hand at me.

"I think it's this whole reunion thing. Making all the games for the grandbabies, and making sure we have enough food for the immense amount of people that we have, it's just adding up."

"I suppose it is."

She shrugged and gave me a soft smile. "I love our family, but we do tend to procreate often."

I snorted.

"You had five kids Mom. Seriously?"

"I know it's my fault. I'm the one who decided to have two sets of twins, rather than just one set like my brother."

"You are an overachiever."

"It's true. I can't help it."

She grinned at me and I snorted.

"Well, all the invites are out, and that took forever."

"Tell me about it. Because we couldn't just send an invite to each household, we had invite each Montgomery, as well as those that are married into the family."

"That's only a few hundred."

"You joke, but we will have well over one hundred people at this event."

I winced, then looked around the immense backyard that my parents had created, that my landscape-architect brother Benjamin had helped build.

"We're going to fit them all?"

"We will. It won't even be a tight fit, but it will feel a little ridiculous."

"Are any of the extra family members coming?"

"The ones that we've basically absorbed over the years? A few. For instance, a couple of Eliza's brothers are going to join, and even help out."

"Because they have that business in Texas?"

"Yes, so they have the experience. And then a few other larger families are coming. Like your cousin Liam's wife, Arden? She has a few brothers that live in Boulder, and they are coming with their families. And so on and so on."

I rolled my eyes. "In other words, we'll basically have the population of an entire small country for this."

"Pretty much."

"Well, it's going to be amazing."

"It should be. We have the food all planned, since we are catering it."

"I know you wanted to do the cooking on your own. Or at least with your sisters-in-law."

She waved me off. "When it was just the four of us, it was easier to do, and then we got married and had children of our own. Then we could still somewhat work within the confines of cooking for ourselves. Although, the fact that my brother had eight kids really did tilt the curve there."

I snorted. "And you with a measly five."

"Well, we can't help that." She waved me off. "But when everyone's children's children started to arrive, it got a little crazy. Leif is the oldest one now, and he's what, twenty?" She frowned. "I can't remember. I'm going to have to look at my calendar. I've had to make a spreadsheet of grandbabies, and eventually great-grandbabies, so I don't miss birthdays or other life events."

"It gets a little ridiculous."

"Yes, but I love it." She reached forward and squeezed my hand. "Thank you for helping me with all of this. I know we have a few things to go over with the caterer and the other event coordinators, but I love that you are helping. And I just want you to know that I didn't invite you to help me with this because you were the only one that wasn't married and without kids."

Ice slid over me. "Oh?"

"Don't say that. I know you thought that, and I tried to make sure you understood that it wasn't that way, but I don't think you believed me."

"It makes sense though. Everybody has new babies, infants that aren't sleeping through the night yet."

"And each one has helped me. Or I could have gotten one of your cousins to help, or my siblings. There were so many other options, but I chose you because I wanted to spend time with my son. Because I love you, and with you working outside the business slightly, and everything with Marc, I just wanted to see you more. Your father and I are trying to spend more time with each of you. Because life is short, and I don't want to miss out on anything."

I swallowed hard and pressed my lips together. I didn't like her talking about time being finite. I didn't like the idea of losing her. Losing any of them. Our family was big, and that meant we loved hard, but we also grieved harder. I didn't want to think about what could happen in the next ten, twenty years. I was just now finding my happiness again, and I hadn't even had a child yet. Something I had always wanted.

But what was I supposed to do? Run from what would make me happy? Run from what could hurt?

I didn't know, but as I held my mom's hand, I let out a deep breath, and tried not to choke up on emotion.

"I love you, Mom. And I love this time that we're spending together."

"Speaking of love," she hedged, and I narrowed my eyes at her.

"Mom."

"I'm just saying. I did invite Killian to the reunion. Just in case you didn't."

She started to move papers around as if she hadn't just tried to throw my world into chaos, and I laughed.

"He told me."

"He did?" she asked brightly.

"After I invited him. I thought it was a big move, inviting him to the reunion."

"It is. And I'm so proud of you. That's why I invited him."

"Because you wanted to throw me into a big move?" I asked, confused.

"No. So that way he could come as just a friend in case it was too much for you. But I thought you would want him here. I see the way you two look at each other."

"Mom. You know he's been through a lot."

"You have too."

"Yes, but he's still going through his. So we're going slow."

"You two are spending practically every night together, even with the drive." She paused, then looked up at me. "Are you going to move?" she asked, her voice low.

I bit my lip. "Mom, we're not ready for that."

"That's not a no." She sighed. "If it happened, at least you would be in the same state. I've been very lucky that my babies have all decided to stay here, and work together, for as long as they have. We are not Fort Collins Montgomery Builders, we are Montgomery Builders. So I suppose you being in a different city, even as close as it is, is something I might have to deal with."

"Mom. We aren't ready for that. Things are getting complicated, not just with what I may or may not be feeling with Killian, but just life in general. Can we just worry about the reunion?"

Because I didn't know what I wanted. That house still spoke to me, but I didn't want Killian to think I wanted a house because of him. It might be a side benefit, but even saying that felt wrong. I hadn't put an offer in yet, Robert and Evelyn hadn't put the place on the market yet, either. Moving out there would change everything. Would I still be able to work at Montgomery Builders? I didn't think so. We were a family owned and operated company. Yes we brought in other members that became family, but all of my siblings worked there. I couldn't just change it.

I wasn't sure what to do, or to think, so I let out a breath and pushed those thoughts away. I didn't have time for that. I had just come to terms with the fact that I loved Killian.

I didn't want to scare him by telling him my feelings.

I had done that once, with Marc. And he had said it back, and now I was still afraid he had said it only to placate me.

That he had married me only to do the same.

So, I wasn't going to do that again. I wasn't going to put the cart before the horse and worry about my job, my livelihood, my home, or Killian.

I would just spend this time with my mom. Because time *was* finite and I needed to enjoy the moment. At least, that's what I kept telling myself.

Chapter Seventeen

Killian

Once again, the breeze slid through my hair and I rolled my shoulders back, kneeling down in front of the two gravestones that spoke to me in whispers and memories.

"I've come out here more often recently. I don't know if it's to say goodbye or just to tell you about my day. I like the drive, so does Cora." I looked over at Cora, who I had decided after a long moment to bring with me. She lay near Cassidy's grave, her head on her paw as she stared off into the distance.

My heart clutched, and I had to wonder if maybe she knew. What was I saying? Of course, Cora knew. That dog knew me better than anyone, maybe even better than Archer.

"Cora's here. As you know. I've been taking good care of her, Cassidy. You always told me that I would want a dog and that I'd be the best doggy dad, just like I was the best little-girl dad. And I think I'm doing okay." I swallowed the hard knot of emotion as Cora looked up at me, ears perked. "We're doing okay, right, girl?"

I let out a breath, steeling myself.

"I'm doing okay. Promise." I looked at Cora, who seemed to almost nod before putting her head back down on her paw.

I shook my head, my lips twitching into a smile. I was doing that more often than not these days. I wasn't growling as much. I wasn't hiding in my own home. No, I was being me. All because somebody had jumped into my life, fallen right on top of me, and changed everything.

"You would really like him, girls. I think next time I come out here, I'll bring him with me." I rubbed the back of my neck. "I want to believe that you guys would be okay with that. That you would understand. And I think you would. Because you're my family. And I love you just as much now as I did before. I will never understand the whys of it. But I understand that you are gone and that I'm still here. That I don't get to go away and hide from who I was. So, I'm trying my best. And I think Archer's helping." I cleared my throat. "No, I *know* he's helping. I love you guys.

So much. I'm going to do my best to earn his faith in me. And your own." I looked down at my hands and then up at the girls who were no longer here but still a huge part of my life.

"I love him." I hadn't meant to say the words out loud, but now that they were there, I knew they were true.

"I love him so much. And I didn't mean to fall for him. I didn't mean to fall for anyone. I thought you were my forever, Danielle. I was ready to spend the rest of my life with you, and the world didn't see fit to allow that to happen. And so I hid. I fought. I did everything I could not to let it happen."

I wiped away a tear.

"Now I have to move on. Not without you, because you'll always be here. Part of this. But Archer knows about you. Knows I'm still in pain. But that I'm healing. And he's helping. So, I don't know if I can ask you for permission because I don't know if it works like that. But I hope you could be happy for me. I just wish that you were here, girls. I love you so fucking much. I probably shouldn't curse, especially around Cassidy, but you'll have to forgive me, babe."

"There's a lot of things that you need forgiveness for," Branson growled out from behind me and I turned, the hairs on the back of my neck standing on end at the sound of my former father-in-law's voice.

He stood there in his crisp jeans, cowboy boots, and his Stetson. He'd let his white handlebar mustache grow out a bit, looking far more shaggy than I had ever seen it. His skin was tan from all the years out in the sun on the ranch, and I didn't think he looked happy. But then again, he never had. Even when he'd had his family still around him.

Danielle's mother had died right after Cassidy had been born, and after losing the girls, it was just Branson and Trevor, Danielle's brother.

I didn't see Trevor anymore, and that was on him, not me. Even in my angriest, my most self-destructive, I had tried. For them. I hadn't been enough.

So, Trevor stayed away, and Branson was angry. Every time I came out here, Branson seemed to show up.

And I wasn't sure what to do about that.

"Cora and I are just here to pay our respects."

"Talking about having sex with another man? Loving someone else? No, there's no respect here. You're tarnishing her name with just being here."

"Respectfully, we don't need to do this. You and I have never seen eye to eye. Let's not have this fight here."

"I don't care anymore. Don't fucking care about you."

"Okay then." I looked at Cora, "Let's go, pup." She stood, pressed to my side, and glared at the other man. She didn't growl or bark, but I could feel the tension radiating off her.

"You best keep her away from me. Not in the mood for some mutt."

Cora was a purebred Lab, but that wasn't what

mattered. Cora was a connection to my daughter and wife, connection to Branson, and the man had never seen it. He wanted nothing to do with what he had lost, but still came out to this gravesite. Still clutched dying daisies in his hand.

Because he was grieving too, and even though he hated me, I lived with it.

Because he was hurting.

And I was just learning to heal.

"Goodbye, Branson."

"You were never right for her."

I shook my head as I kept going. "No, I wasn't. But she was mine. If only for a little while." And then I got into my truck, Cora following me, and I headed home, wondering why a man could hate me for so long, and why I let him.

I pulled into the house to see Penny and Archer standing there, smiles on their faces. They were talking, and I opened the door to let Cora out. Before I got out, I waved the two of them off and pulled out my phone.

Today was the day for healing. At least, that's what I told myself. I should start doing it.

I pressed the contact in my phone, holding my breath, hoping I wasn't making a mistake.

"Killian? Are you okay? You haven't called me in over three years. It's always me calling you. Oh my God. Is this Killian?"

"Ann, you're talking so fast I can barely understand you."

"It's you. Is everything okay?" She choked on a sob, and I cursed under my breath.

I had not reached out to my sister since I lost my family. I was hurting the family I had left because I was in pain. Because I was a fucking asshole.

But no longer. I looked up at Archer as he gave me a look, and I smiled at him, seeing the worry and relief mingled in his gaze.

He was healing, so I needed to heal, too. Damn it.

"I just wanted to hear your voice. And to actually call. Because I haven't done that."

"Oh." And then she promptly burst into tears.

Ann's husband picked up the phone and whispered words to her that I couldn't quite catch, other than that they were something sweet.

"Ann has to put her feet up right now. Doctor's orders."

Tension radiated through me. "What?"

"Stop worrying him," my sister called out from the background.

"I can get on a flight right now if you need me."

There was too much silence. I was afraid that the call had been disconnected. Instead, my brother-in-law cleared his throat.

"You should come out and visit. See your family. We want to come out there too. We're just giving you space. Ann's okay. I shouldn't have mentioned the doctor's orders so quickly since it's not serious yet. I'm just fucking terrified."

Alarm shot through me, and my hands shook. "I'll head down there right now."

"Let's make plans so you can come and visit. And not out of worry or fear."

"But she's okay. Is my sister okay?" My hands went clammy, my mouth dry.

There was a scramble, and then the phone went to speakerphone, as Ann berated her husband softly.

"I'm really okay. The doctor said I just needed to take it easy. I'm not on bed rest, and I can still do what I normally did. I just need to stop stressing out."

Only a small amount of relief hit me, and I let out a shaky breath. "I'm not going to be that stress for you anymore. Okay?"

"Okay. If you do this for me, I will love you forever."

"You'll love me forever no matter what. I've learned that over the past few years."

"Killian," she cried, as my brother-in-law whispered sweet words to her.

"We're okay here. Was there a reason that you called?" he asked, and I could hear the tension in his voice.

I remembered when Danielle had been pregnant, how worried I was about every single little thing. How the unknown was the most terrifying thing about it.

And how I could do nothing. In the end, I couldn't do anything anyway, but I had tried.

I kept trying.

I should continue to do so. Or at least do better about it.

"I just wanted to call because I hadn't. And I will come down and visit. Soon. We'll make plans." I cleared my throat. "Probably after the Montgomery family reunion because I want to bring Archer."

There was clapping and cheers, and I heard my brother-in-law chuckle. "Well, you made my wife happy. So I guess I'm in your debt."

"No. I'm forever in yours. Both of you. Thank you for being good to me. After all this time when I was pulling away. Thanks for not giving up."

"I'm really going to need to meet this Archer," Ann cried.

"Me too," my brother-in-law grumbled.

"Let's make plans. I'll talk to Archer, and the four of us can figure it out."

"That sounds wonderful," Ann hiccupped, and I smiled into the phone.

"I love you. All of you. And I'll see you soon."

We said our goodbyes and they hung up. I turned to see Archer standing at my open door staring at me, tears freely flowing down his face.

"So, I'm going to Texas?" he asked as he shook his head. "Do I get to wear chaps? I feel like I need to wear chaps."

I rolled my eyes, leaned out the open door, and kissed him hard on the mouth. "You're more likely to wear chaps and cowboy hats out here, this close to Wyoming."

"And there are more cowboys in Texas in my head. At least, that's what romance novels told me."

"I need to read these novels," I whispered.

"Maybe."

"If you two are done being adorably adorable over there, I brought the fixings for dinner, but I want you to make it."

"What am I making?" I called out, laughing at Penny's antics.

"Asparagus and chicken lemon stir-fry, with sticky rice, and buns."

"I'm doing all that, am I?" I asked, my eyes wide.

"I can help. It's super easy. Just sort of mix everything together on high heat."

"Okay. I guess we're having stir-fry tonight."

Cora barked, and I shook my head. "Not for you. Remember the last time you had asparagus, Cora?"

Somehow my dog looked a little contrite before she bounced around Penny.

I looked at the family I was making and figured, fuck, I'm doing this right.

"So, you went up to Wyoming?" Archer asked later as we were getting ready for bed. Dinner had been filling, tasty, and we'd only almost caught the kitchen on fire once.

I counted that as a win, and as Cora padded around the bedroom trying to find a place to get comfortable since she liked to sleep in different places each night, I just smiled.

"Just to say goodbye."

Archer froze looked up at me. "Oh?"

"I used to go to tell them about my day, to rage, to say I was sorry. And maybe I still will, but today I mostly talked about you."

I looked up at him then, hoping he could sense what was inside me because I couldn't say it. The fact that I had said it out loud to my girls was one thing. Saying it to Archer was a completely different thing. And I didn't know if I was ready yet.

But I would be.

The fact that I even acknowledged it was a step. I just had to hope Archer would be okay with that.

"All good things, I hope. Unless you're telling them how I like to take over the bed and sleep like a starfish." He blushed. "Or maybe you don't tell your daughter that."

"I have not explained that, but I'm sure they know how much I care about you."

Archer opened his mouth to say something, then shook his head. "You're going to make me cry, and I don't know if I want to cry again."

"I've been doing enough of that for the past few years, even when I don't want to. I understand."

"Thank you. For telling me."

"I told them I would bring you with me next time." I let out a breath at Archer's stunned look. "And bring you down to meet my sister and her family."

"I guess it's only fair since you've met mine, and will meet the rest of them soon."

"Even if I hadn't, Archer, I'd want you to meet them. Because you're important to me."

"You're important to me too, Killian."

We got into bed, each wearing pajama bottoms and soft T-shirts. There would be no sex tonight, maybe in the morning when we woke up, but for now, we were just comfortable. I had work to do on the house in the morning, and Archer had work to do at the house next door, hence why he was spending the night again even if we weren't doing more than sleeping.

But this was comfortable, and as Cora wiggled her body in between us, I laughed and cuddled my dog and my man and told myself that this was good. We were doing okay.

* * *

When I woke up the next morning, the sun shining in the room, I looked at Archer sleeping softly, his mouth parted slightly, and Cora still between us and snoring louder than either of us.

I laughed, I couldn't help it, and as I kept laughing I shook the bed slightly, waking Archer up.

"I don't know. I think you may snore louder than her."

I froze and glared at him.

"You're lucky I love you, Montgomery. Those are fighting words."

Archer's eyes widened, but I didn't mind. I hadn't known how I was going to tell him, how I should, but I knew Archer was holding back. I could tell. Of course, I could tell. So I had to be the one to say it first. It was only right. And, fuck, I wanted to.

"Oh. Well, same then. You're lucky I love you, too."

Cora wiggled between us as she stood up and began to pace around the bottom of the bed, and I used that moment to lean forward and kiss Archer gently on the mouth, and then a little harder.

"It's a little early, but I guess we can get ready for the day."

"I hope so. I have a couple of meetings, and I want to go to the storage unit and get more of my stuff."

"Stuff from the other house? From up north?"

I nodded as we both stretched and watched Cora pace. I figured I needed to take her out soon.

"Yeah. All the stuff from the other house. Things that I kept of Danielle's and Cassidy's."

"I can help if you want. If you can wait till after I'm done with what I need to do at the other house. If you want help."

"I love you, Archer. So yes. We should go through some of those boxes together. I want you to know them."

"I want to know them too."

I frowned as my eyes began to water, and a scent of smoke hit my nose.

"What the fuck is that?"

And then Cora began to bark as smoke billowed out from under the doorway.

"Holy hell. Is that fire?" Archer asked as we leapt out of bed, and my worst fears began to slam into me.

The house was on fire.

And we were trapped.

Chapter Eighteen

Killian

The car slammed into the ice, screams echoing through my brain as everything happened so quickly. I turned to see Danielle, her eyes wide, as we scrambled to try to get out of the car. Danielle worked her seatbelt, trying to get the lever, but everything was hazy. She put her hand up to her head, blood pouring down from a wound.

But that wasn't right. Danielle hadn't moved. She had hit her head on the side of the car, the airbags not deploying, and she hadn't moved.

That much I remembered.

And I hadn't heard a scream, not after we hit the ice.

Water filled the car, but there were no screams, nothing, just ice and cold and nothing.

Heat blasted against my face as someone gripped my arms.

"Killian."

There was a bark, then another, a frantic wail, and I looked down at Cora, then at Archer, and cursed under my breath. "The house is on fire."

"I know. Are you with me?"

He looked at me then, his gaze earnest, and I nodded. "I've got you. You have to get out of here."

"We can't. This door is locked, the doorknob's hot, but we'll try the other door."

"Get Cora."

"I've got her. We've got this."

Smoke billowed around us and I coughed, leaning Archer towards me as the house began to shake. The house was still under construction and we were on a hill. If we weren't careful, the whole damn thing was going to fall down on top of us.

"We've got to get out of here," I shouted over the sound of fire and snapping wood. I pulled a towel out from underneath the rack, slid it over Archer's head, and pulled Cora towards me.

"We've got it. Let's go!"

Archer nodded, fear in his gaze. I was right there with him.

We wore no shoes, thin pajamas, Cora was barking, and all I could do was try to get us out of here.

I pressed my hand to the other door that went to the sunroom and felt no heat.

The door was locked from the outside and I cursed under my breath.

"It's locked."

"But the lock is on the inside!" Archer coughed.

I cursed again, then slammed my shoulder into the door.

"Stay back, hold Cora."

Archer nodded, then lifted Cora up because she was shaking on her three legs. I tried to suck in a breath, then rammed my body into the door, once, twice, over and over. The door splintered, and I swallowed hard before pulling them behind me.

"Watch out for the shards."

Archer coughed again. "I've got Cora. She's safe."

I needed to make sure they were both safe.

"Stop right there," a very familiar voice said far too calmly from in front of us, and the sound of the gun cocking sent chills down my body.

"Trevor?" I asked, my voice croaking. And not just because of the smoke.

My brother-in-law snarled in front of me, the gun in his hand sending cold chills down my body and through my soul. "You think you can just live after what you did? You killed my sister. You killed her! You killed her little girl. And you think you get to just live free, as if you didn't do anything? As if you didn't sacrifice them so you could have this house and this money? Well, fuck you."

"Could we maybe talk about this outside of the burning building?" Archer asked, holding a sixty-pound dog in his arms.

I didn't think Archer could see the gun, and I knew he was scared, hence the sarcasm, but I needed to protect my family.

There was broken glass and shards of wood everywhere, and though I knew mine and Archer's feet were probably bleeding, he was still holding our damn dog to make sure she was safe.

Cora was growling, wiggling, but Archer kept still as I moved to the side to put my body between us.

"Just let them go. We can talk about this," I said as calmly as I could.

"Fuck you. You just show up here with a fucking man that you're screwing in your marriage bed. And you think this is okay? My dad says that you just show up at the grave-yard like you have the right to. Have the right to come to her side and talk to her as if you matter. You killed her, and you have the audacity to be here?"

"Trevor. We need to get out of this building. It's not safe."

"You built it. It's probably just going to kill your little lover over there just like you killed your wife. That's what they're going to say, you know. That you were worthless, that just like you killed your wife, my goddam sister, you killed your lover because you can't even build a house correctly. It's your fault the wiring was screwed up. It's your fault that the windows kept breaking, that the structural integrity isn't there."

Of course, it was Trevor this whole time. Not some kids, not some hiker who wanted to screw with my property.

It was Trevor. He literally hated me that much. But I had hated myself for far longer, and I refused to let Cora or Archer get hurt because of this man.

"It's between you and me. Let them go."

"Killian," Archer snapped as he set Cora down, holding her collar. She barked, pulling at the collar, and when Trevor lowered the gun towards her, I screamed, my body shaking with rage.

"Don't you dare!"

The gun went off as I moved, pushing towards Trevor. Archer shouted, throwing his body over the dog as Cora moved between all of us, barking and snapping her teeth.

Trevor screamed as Cora lunged. I looked around for blood but only saw the few cuts on our feet. The gun had gone off, but the bullet had embedded into the wall behind us.

But the fire was still going, the smoke still billowing, and I cursed, pulling Cora off Trevor.

"We've got to go."

"I can't just leave him here," I spat, and I met Archer's gaze.

"Okay. Let's go."

I tugged Trevor out by his waistband as he glared at me, throwing a fist. I punched him back, slamming my fist into his face. "Don't you fucking dare."

"You killed her! You killed my sister. Fuck you."

It was as if the other man had nothing else to say, but I didn't care. I refused to let Danielle's brother die for his own hatred, as long as I could keep my family safe.

"We have to get out of here. I'm not going to die for you."

"You should have died along with her. You were the one driving. It was your fault."

I coughed, my body shaking as embers began to fall on us. "Trevor! The road was slick, and another car came at us. I will regret every day of my life that I wasn't good enough to stay on the road. That I was the one that they pulled out, that they didn't pull my little girl out or my wife out in time. I know they're gone. I will always blame myself, but I'm here. We are both still here, living." *For now.* "Don't ruin that."

"Screw you."

He reached out again, trying to punch me and I ducked, pulling Trevor with me as part of a roof caved in.

Archer screamed, and there were more shouts, sirens, Cora barking. But I couldn't breathe, the smoke getting to be too much. I crawled, trying to take Trevor with me, but he was out cold, either the smoke or part of the roof caving in hit him on the head. But he had to be breathing. He had to be all right. I began to crawl, trying to pull myself out, trying to do anything.

And then Archer was there, pulling on my arms.

"Killian. We have to go."

There was fear in his gaze, his blue eyes wild, and I nodded tightly.

"Trevor."

"There are others here. I'll get him."

As I let Archer pull me out, I reached around and gripped Trevor by the arm.

"Both of us."

"Oh, fuck, okay. Hold tight."

Archer pulled, tugged, then the firemen came, shouting out orders. I had Trevor, and then they took him away from me, and I fell into Archer's arms.

Blood poured from a wound on my forehead and soot-covered us both. Our feet were bleeding, and Cora was barking all around us, but we were holding each other, and people were moving us away, the fire engulfing the house.

As we moved far away enough to be safe, I looked at the place, my eyes wide.

Someone was saying something to me, trying to put an oxygen mask over me, but I could only just stare. Stare at the place that had been the home I was building for my family, the family that wasn't coming back.

And now it was gone, too.

Archer slid his hand into mine as he breathed into his own oxygen mask. Someone else was taking care of Cora near us, using a pet oxygen mask that they'd pulled out of their truck.

I just stood there.

"It's gone. All of it's gone." I coughed as the paramedic put the oxygen mask back on my face.

"I'm sorry, baby," Archer whispered.

I just shook my head and leaned into him as I watched the rest of my place burn. The forest around it would be safe, thanks to the firemen protecting the land and the people.

But my home was gone.

And I could only hold on to Archer, and then Cora, and then Penny as she came to us, and knew that a part of my life was over.

I didn't know what I was supposed to do.

I looked over to where Trevor was being wheeled into an ambulance, and I had to wonder if that could have been me —if the hate and damage to my heart could have turned me into that.

"Don't think it. It wasn't you."

I looked down at Archer as he sat at the back of another ambulance, glaring at me.

"Stop reading my mind," I whispered.

"It's the only thing I can do when you don't talk to me."

"Neither one of you should be talking because you're supposed to have the oxygen masks on your faces," Penny snapped, as the paramedic gave her a kind smile.

"Now, both of you go get checked out and cleaned up. I will take care of Cora."

"Penny," I whispered.

"No, keep that oxygen mask on. We will deal with all of this. Me and Archer's family. We've got this."

Archer's eyes widened, and she narrowed her gaze.

"Yes, I called your mother. Get over it. They will meet you at the hospital. Apparently, this is something you guys do often as a family, because she had a whole system."

Archer smiled softly, and I looked at my family, the one I was making, and then back at the house that was turning to embers and ashes.

Everything I built was gone, but I would find a way to rebuild.

Somehow.

And with Archer by my side and the family we were making, I figured that maybe, just maybe, we would be okay.

Chapter Nineteen

Archer

My body ached, but it was finally for a good reason.

I looked up at Killian as he brushed a kiss against my lips, and I ran my hands over his shoulders and down his back to grip his ass.

"You taste like perfection," he whispered, and I smiled up at him.

"You keep stealing my lines." I leaned forward to kiss him softly, and then he kissed me back, this time a little harder, his tongue sliding against my lips. I opened for him, aching for him.

"Archer. I need you."

"You already have me."

He lowered himself towards me and slowly began to enter me. I tensed slightly and forced myself to relax, the feeling just on that side of sweet pain that was exactly what we both wanted. It was sweet, loving, and then we turned over and I rode him. I leaned down, took his lips, and came along with him, both of us shaking, our hands tangling with one another as we leaned into each other.

"Good morning," he whispered as he kissed me softly and slid his hands down my side. I winced, and his eyes went cloudy.

"I'm fine. I'm all healed."

"You still have a bruise there."

I shook my head and gripped his face with both hands. "It's healing. I'm just still a little tender yet."

"We shouldn't be doing this."

I swallow hard and shook my head. "We're doing exactly what we need to. Come on, stop freaking out. We're both okay. Cora is okay. Penny is doing great. Today's a big day. Let's not worry about anything else."

"I can't believe I almost lost you both. You and Cora." His eyes went cloudy again, and I ran my hands through his hair, both of us naked under the blankets, just quietly taking our time that morning.

"You have a few cuts and bruises, more than me. I'm fine. Cora is better than fine."

"Because you took care of her," Killian whispered.

I shrugged and played with the feather from the down pillow that had fallen on top of Killian's shoulder.

"We're healthy, and right where we need to be."

Killian sat up in bed, and I did my best to keep my gaze from the way his muscles moved while he stretched and flexed. "I don't like it. I don't like the fact that somebody from my past, somebody that blames me for so much, hurt you."

"He hurt *you*." I sat up and rubbed my hand down his back. He still had a few cuts, abrasions, and bruises, but they were healing.

In the week-and-a-half since the fire, we were still healing and Killian had moved in with me in my small apartment in Fort Collins. Cora enjoyed herself, though I knew she would rather have been out in the open than in a small complex.

Every single one of my siblings and even a few of my cousins had offered to take them in as well so Cora could have more space, but the three of us needed to be together. As the family that we were slowly becoming.

"He's going to jail for a long time. And maybe he'll finally get the help that he needs," I said after a moment.

"I knew he hated me. Just the way Branson hates me. But I never thought that they would stoop to this. I always thought that they would do their best to push me out of visiting their graves. Not this."

"They're hurting, and while I don't know if I can forgive Trevor for hurting you the way he did, I can understand that he was going through so much and didn't handle it well."

I winced as Killian turned his head and raised an

eyebrow at me. "I see that we're doing well with the whole denial thing. Thank you for trying."

I snorted. I couldn't help it. "I'm not very good at this."

"You're the best at it, Archer."

We both sat there a minute, and then he let out a breath. "You do know what yesterday was, don't you?"

I frowned and shook my head. "Today's the reunion, so what am I missing?"

Killian let out a laugh before Cora let herself into the bedroom, having learned how to open the doors if we didn't lock them.

The dog bounded on the bed and I rolled my eyes.

"You're such a smart girl. You're the best girl." She licked my chin and then sat on my lap as if she wasn't a sixty-pound Lab.

"Yesterday was Marc's wedding."

I froze and Cora whined. I shook myself out of it and rubbed her down, letting her know that she was indeed the best girl ever.

"I forgot." I shook my head, stunned. "*I forgot.*"

"Of course you did. Because I'm the one that's the most important." Killian fluttered his eyelashes, and it wasn't the most attractive thing on him since he was overexaggerating so much, so I just laughed.

"I guess that tells you where he lies in the grand scheme of things."

"I'm just glad that he seems to have moved on because he didn't call you. Didn't bother you at all."

"Which is good. Apparently all it takes to find someone that's worth it is me throwing myself off a roof to catch a man's attention."

Killian scowled. "You'll not be falling off any more roofs, even if I'm there to catch you. I don't think I could handle that."

"Okay. That makes sense. So, you think you're ready to talk about what you're going to do with the place?"

"Yes, but I have an idea about it that may not be what you're thinking."

I frowned. "What do you mean?"

"I'm going to rebuild, but something a little different. However, I think we need to talk with your family first."

I froze. "What do you mean?"

Killian shook his head. "Let's get ready for the reunion and then head to your mother's house. We can talk about it with them."

"Killian. I'm nervous now."

"We should buy the house you're building, too. To have them both. Because that house calls to you, and I don't know if I could live at the other place again. But I also don't want to get rid of the land. So, let's figure out something that can work for the both of us."

"You're not making any sense."

Killian met my gaze and cupped my face. "I want to spend the rest of my life with you, Archer. If that means moving to Fort Collins, I'll do it, but that house calls to you.

Not the house I was building for Danielle and Cassidy. But the house you're building. Let's try to make that work."

"I don't know if we can."

"I think you need to talk with your family."

"And today's the best day to do that?" I asked, my mind whirling in a thousand different directions.

"You never know. Those Montgomerys do like to plan things. Let's see what they've already set in motion before we stress ourselves out."

"You're stressing me out, Killian."

"Well, considering you fell on me after falling off a roof, it's only right."

"You want to spend the rest of your life with me?" I asked, freezing as his words just caught up to me.

Killian looked over his shoulder at me as he began walking naked towards the bathroom. It was really hard not to look at his ass just then, but this was important.

"Yes. So, let's figure out exactly what that means. Now, go feed our dog while I shower. Because if we do that together, we're never making it to your mother's house."

I laughed, not knowing I would be able to after everything that had happened, but from the light in Killian's eyes, I knew he felt the same way.

We were finding our future, somehow. But what did that mean?

* * *

We got ready quickly and made our way to my parents' house. Thankfully, Killian was the same size as Beckett, so instead of having to buy a whole new wardrobe right away, he was able to borrow some clothes, including the pair of gray pants and a button-up shirt he had on.

"Oh, I'm so glad that you're here. This is exciting," my mother said as she looked around her house, beaming. My mother and father had gone all out for this. The reunion would start a bit later, but first the Fort Collins Montgomerys were going to get ready as a family before the rest of the horde arrived.

We had opened up the back windows so the deck was fully visible, having pulled back the French doors, so everything looked open and welcoming. Today was the best weather we'd had in weeks, as if Mother Nature knew the Montgomerys needed this.

The lawn tables were set up outside underneath tents with fairy lights, and there was a gaming section and a dance floor, everything perfectly situated, so it looked more like a casual wedding rather than a family reunion.

I was just excited to see everybody, especially with how my mother smiled.

"It looks beautiful."

"You did so much work with me. I love you, my son," Mom said as she kissed both cheeks.

Dad came into the room then, holding a stack of boxes. "Where do you want these, babe?" Dad asked before he looked over her head and smiled at me.

"Archer, Killian, you're here. Is Cora with you?" At that moment, Cora barked, and Dad grinned. "I'm glad we made sure all the pets were allowed to come if they were comfortable. And Cora is such a well-behaved dog. She's like a grandkid."

He winked as he said it, and Killian let out a low breath.

"Well, that was pointed."

"He's getting good at it. Usually, it's just Mom."

"We try, honey," Mom said. "Now, let me go help your dad with those boxes, and you go take a look around. You know what you're doing."

"Yes, he does," Annabelle said as she walked in, Hailey in her arms. Jacob was behind her, Jack in his arms. And then Benjamin and Brenna were there, Rafael in Brenna's arms. Beckett and Eliza followed, holding Lexington. And Paige and Lee came in last, with Emery sleeping in Lee's arms.

I looked at my family and just shook my head. Somehow our huge family became even more extensive, and I wasn't sure how it happened. But I loved it. Everybody was growing up and having kids and just having a life that they'd always wanted.

I could barely keep everything in.

The doorbell rang again, and then Clay walked in without us even having to answer, since he was family.

"You're here," Mom said as she pulled the gift out of his hand, handed it over to Dad, and hugged him tight.

Riggs, Clay's husband, smiled from behind Clay and then was enveloped in the hug as well.

Jackson, Holden, and Mariah, Clay's cousins, the ones that he had been raising for years now as his own, piled into the house. They were laughing, talking a mile a minute, as everybody wrapped around each other, switching off babies, the noise intensifying.

And this was just the Fort Collins branch.

I knew it was just going to get even louder as each set of the Montgomerys walked in.

"Okay, before the rest of the family gets here, we have an announcement and an idea," Beckett said as he looked over at his twin, and I froze.

"What's going on? An announcement?" Everyone else seemed to know what was going on, and I wasn't a fan of being left out.

"Oh yes, you're going to be really excited about this," Paige said as she clapped her hands, and Annabelle grinned.

"I don't think I like the fact that the four of you know this and I don't."

Clay came up to me, his eyes wide. "Should I be here for this?"

"Hold me," I said, and Clay did indeed wrap his arms around me, and both Riggs and Killian just laughed.

"We have an idea. So maybe we should have just said *idea*," Paige began, bouncing.

Beckett held up his hand, his eyes filled with laughter. "Let me do this since I think Paige had around five cups of coffee."

"Six," she muttered.

Lee winced. "I don't know if she's joking."

"Anyway," Beckett continued. "As you know, Montgomery Builders is getting bigger. We have more partners coming in, and we've had to turn away clients."

I nodded as Clay moved so we were holding hands, and he squeezed mine.

I looked over at my friend, and Clay just beamed. "I have no idea what's going on, but I feel like things are about to change."

"Change can be good," Riggs whispered, and Killian nodded. The four of us stood shoulder to shoulder as the rest of the adults looked at us. I had a feeling they all knew what was going on while we didn't.

Nervous didn't even begin to encapsulate it.

"Because of that, we have an *idea*," Beckett continued. "We would like to open up another branch of Montgomery Builders closer to Boulder, because we've been getting so many offers for that area. We've talked about this before in passing, but we're serious now. And since Colorado is growing so much, we feel like it's a good time to expand. And, because of that, we would like the Boulder branch to be run by two people we think can handle it. They can work at both branches, just like we will, but there would be two people in charge of it."

I blinked, my mind slow to catch up.

"Are you shitting me?" Clay exclaimed and then blushed. "Sorry. I didn't curse. Don't listen to that, kids."

"We heard," Clay's oldest shouted from the other side of the room.

"You want to open another branch?" I asked, ignoring the laughter from both sides of the room.

"I know it's crazy," Annabelle said as she held up both hands. "But you were even with us when we talked about this at first."

"Yes, and I thought Clay and our seconds-in-command would run the place if it actually happened. You want me to go?" I asked, not knowing if the excitement of being close to Killian or the feeling of being pushed out was the biggest emotion within me.

"Archer," Annabelle whispered as she came to me. I let go of Clay's and Killian's hands as she slid her hands into mine. "I love you. And if you hadn't been spending so much time at the Boulder house with Killian and with your team there, I wouldn't even have allowed this to become an option." My twin winked. "But we will always work as a family. These two branches will work as one. I will be over at the Boulder branch often, all of us will. Because we need to train our counterparts so that way we work as a cohesive unit. I think this is good for you. This way, we're still working as a family, but there are no choices to be made. We can have the best of both worlds."

Benjamin added more details, but I felt like I was barely keeping up.

"You're not kicking me out." I hadn't even known I was voicing the words until they spilled out of my mouth.

"For fuck's sake, we don't want to kick you out," Beckett growled, then winced. "Sorry, kids."

"We still heard you," Clay's middle kid said, and everyone laughed.

"We're not kicking you out," Beckett repeated. "We're just growing so we can include the entire family. And that includes Clay. He'll have the same position that I do, and he's basically a fucking Montgomery. I know I'm cursing. Just let it happen."

"I can't believe this." I looked over at Killian, who just grinned. "Did you know?"

"No, but it goes with what I wanted to talk about this morning."

"It's fate then," Paige said as she clapped her hands. "Nobody will have to choose. Yes, it may be more of a drive some days, but frankly, our projects are moving further and further out from where our main office is anyway. It's going to take at least a year for all of this to happen, and this is just at the idea stage, but it makes sense to us. You don't have to move if you don't want to, but if you do, then we have a plan. If this isn't what you want, then we will come up with another one. Montgomery Builders is family, and our family is growing, so the company should grow."

I wiped tears, not even aware I was crying. "So, we're going to do this."

"We should. We can talk about it, go over details, figure it out." Paige winced as she looked over at us. "Of course, we started to come up with this idea before the fire. So things have changed completely on that front. Ignore us."

Killian shook his head. "I was just telling Archer that he needs to buy the house he's working on since the couple is pretty much building everything to his specs."

I blushed. "I can't help it if I have good taste."

"Well, you have great taste," Annabelle whispered. "And we'll figure things out. But we just wanted to let you know this is an option. That we're always going to be family. We will work together. But now we can make it work for everyone."

I looked at everybody and then held up my arms. Somehow my siblings and I were all hugging, my parents included. And then the spouses and Killian were there, and then the kids, and there was laughter, love, tears. When the doorbell rang and the first set of Denver Montgomerys began to arrive, I knew we could do this.

We were a family. Loud, larger than life.

But we had each other.

And maybe it had taken a while for me to understand that after thinking I had lost everything.

But I had everyone.

I looked over at Killian, the man I loved more than anything, and smiled.

I had Killian. Family. And a future with potential.

I had everything. Finally.

Chapter Twenty

Killian

Archer had often mentioned the size of his family, and the joke among the Montgomerys was that they could take over the world.

I thought he'd been exaggerating.

But, as I looked at the cheese table that was currently being devoured as if a plague of locusts had attacked it, only to be refilled again with the secondary cheese selections, I realized he'd been telling the truth.

"They do love their cheese, don't they?" Lee asked, his voice as awestruck as mine.

"You've known these people for years. You should be used to this by now."

"I've known the Fort Collins Montgomerys for years. You add in the other four branches, and then there are other cousins that don't even live in Colorado, and things get a little insane."

I slowly turn to Lee, my eyes wide with shock. "There are more of them than this?" I held my hand out, encompassing the over one hundred people in the backyard that had the last name Montgomery, and just shook my head slowly.

"Yes, they are related to Archer and the rest from their dad's side. Not their mom's."

"My God," I muttered, and Lee just laughed.

"You get used to it. Maybe. I'm figuring it out."

"I'm sorry I left you alone," Archer said, nearly panting as he ran across the massive backyard that Benjamin had landscaped to perfection. "Got caught up with one of my uncles." He pointed over to a man with a big beard and a large laugh.

"That is Uncle Harry. He is of the Denver branch."

"He's in construction just like your family, right?" I asked. I'm trying to remember everyone.

Archer grinned. "He is. He and my aunt had eight kids."

My mind boggled. "And then there's another set, right?"

"Two more sets. Uncle Harry and Aunt Marie had eight kids. Uncle William and Aunt Katherine had four kids, who all live in Colorado Springs. Uncle Tim and Aunt Francine also had four kids up in Boulder. While my parents had five."

"I can't keep up," I said with a laugh.

"You don't need to. It's why we have name tags."

I looked down at my own name tag that said "Killian, property of Archer Montgomery" and blushed. "Property?"

"It's so that way everyone knows how we're related."

Lee tapped his. "I like being a property of Paige. It's kind of nice."

A woman with dark hair, blunt bangs, and tattooed arms came up to us and beamed. "I like this one," she said as she looked over at Archer.

"Maya," Archer sputtered.

She just winked, unrepentant. "Hi, I'm Maya, one of the Denver cousins. We like you, by the way, Killian. And I remember some of your work from a few years ago."

There was a knowing in her gaze, but she didn't elaborate. Then I snapped my fingers and pointed at her. "You bought our table."

"We did."

"What?" Archer asked, looking between his cousin Maya and me.

"I used to build furniture, remember? Custom furniture."

"He's the hot lumberjack that you bought your table from?" Archer asked Maya, who just smiled wickedly.

"And who I said I should set you up with, but you refused to be set up with anyone, and then well, I didn't realize that you weren't single at the time." Maya straightened, her face draining of color as she turned to me. "I am sorry for your loss. I know today's about joy, but it's also about life. I hope it's okay I brought it up at all."

There was that familiar pain, but I still smiled. "You gave my daughter chocolate. I remember that."

Maya shrugged as Archer slid his hands into mine. "I remember. You need to meet my husbands. I think you'd get along. Oh! And I brought my babies with me, they are over there." She pointed vaguely at the grouping of about fifty small children.

There might have been more, might have been less, I wasn't sure. It was a little hard to keep up. Lee and I were on the periphery, along with some of the other non-Montgomerys who had been invited, where we felt the safest. At least for now.

"Anyway, we love the table, and my sister Miranda has been jealous this whole time that she can never get one."

I frowned. "You know, I could probably work on something. For family."

Maya looked like a cat in cream, but Archer cleared his throat. "You can talk to me about it, I'll be his agent from now on."

"Oh really?" I said with a laugh.

Archer beamed over at me. "Of course. After all, I need to keep our best interests at heart. We're going to have two houses now."

"Two?" Maya said with a gasp and gripped Archer's arm. "Tell me you're buying that house in the woods."

"We're building one, and we're buying the one I'm

working on," Archer said as we both squeezed each other's hands. It had been a quick discussion, but we knew it was exactly what we needed. Two properties, because we had a big family now.

I thought I'd lost everything, and I didn't have the family that I thought I would forever, but now I had more family than I know how to handle.

"Does that mean you're going to let the Montgomerys rent out the spare house?" Maya asked as she rubbed her hands together. "Liam, one of the Boulder Montgomerys, has a cabin in the woods near you, and it's constantly full of Montgomerys and families connected to us."

Archer nodded. "I know. It's a great cabin."

I looked over at Archer. "Really?"

"I'll introduce you. He's over there, the former model."

"Oh yes, I remember the model," I teased, and Maya threw her head back and laughed.

"See? He's perfect for you. Congratulations on the two homes, and I will be first on the list to rent out the spare. Remember, just because we're family doesn't mean we don't pay. We pay our way. We're Montgomerys. Not cheap." She leaned forward and kissed Archer on the cheek, and surprised me by doing the same to me.

"She's amazing," I whispered, and Archer just grinned.

"She is."

Somebody clinked a wine glass and everybody quieted down, even the children and Cora, as well as any other pets that had come. Cora was living in doggy bliss with so many kids who were very gentle with her, as well as other dogs who reveled in the love, including a husky of some sort.

Everybody just looked happy to be there. There was no fighting, just laughs, and maybe some tiffs, but the tension eased quickly.

Archer's mom stood up on the dais, a small stage that they'd had built, which held a microphone and an actual live band that some of the Montgomerys had joined in at some point.

His mother cleared her throat into the mic and waved. "We want to welcome you to the Fort Collins Montgomerys. It's been a long time coming, and we are so happy you're here."

"We're happy we're here," Harry Montgomery of the Denver branch said as he raised his beer.

"I love my family so much. All of my family. All one hundred and twelve of you." Everyone laughed. I was a little worried about that number being true. However, I wasn't about to start counting.

"You've all been eating, enjoying some games, and mingling. Soon we will have our three-legged race and karaoke. Anything we can do just to enjoy each other. We have grandbabies here, and eventually I'm sure we'll have some great-grandbabies." Everyone turned to Leif, the eldest of the Montgomery next generation, and he blushed from head to toe.

"Um, give me a minute or four or ten?" he asked, his voice going high pitched. Everyone laughed, and the kid, who wasn't a kid anymore, ducked behind his big dad. Austin Montgomery laughed and just shook his head.

"Let's wait a while till I'm a grandpa, shall we?" Austin added as everyone laughed some more.

Archer's mom beamed. "Anyway, we are family. We love cheese, games, ink, and working with our hands. Most importantly, we love each other. We have been through more than most, and I don't think it's just because of our numbers. But it's because we face every situation head-on and know that we are the first line of defense of family. I love being a Montgomery. I love the connections that we make and the fact that we are always there for each other." Archer's dad moved forward wrapped his arm around her shoulders as she smiled up at him.

"I've never said I was good at being a Montgomery," Russell Montgomery said with a small laugh as others joined in. "But I've tried my hardest. Especially now that I've watched my kids grow up into the strong and capable human beings that they are. They're bringing into the world a new legacy. Just like all of you are. For those who have decided to have children or those who've decided to be the best aunts and uncles they could be, all of you have shown me what it is to be family. We are all here for each other, no matter what."

Archer leaned into me as he wiped away a tear, and I wrapped my arm around him. Others were tearing up as well, everyone having grouped into their couples or larger family units.

Cora came up to my side, and I ran my hand over her head while she leaned into me.

"Now, today is about family, and not just the family we were born into, the family we have made." Archer's mom looked around at the other couples and triads in the area that weren't Montgomerys by blood, but by friendship and love.

Archer's dad grinned. "Now, enjoy the music, the games, the food, and especially enjoy the cheese. And remember one thing, long live the Montgomerys!"

And as the crowd cheered, I wrapped my arms around Archer and kissed him softly. "Long live the Montgomerys."

"This means you're going to have to get the tattoo," Archer whispered.

"There's a tattoo?" I asked, and as everyone around us laughed, they began to show me exactly where their Montgomery iris was. I had a feeling that even though I hadn't proposed yet, I was now a Montgomery, and that meant anything was possible, and things were just about to change forever.

And I couldn't wait.

Legacy

Leif

"Are you sure that you have everything packed? Your passport, all of your documents? Your itinerary? And you have that little router or wireless thingy so you can have easy access to the internet when you're walking around in Europe, right?" Mom asked as she paced around the room.

I shook my head, and her eyes went wide.

"You don't have that? Oh no. It's okay. We can work through your carry-on together. We've got this."

"Mom. I'm okay. I promise."

Her eyes filled, and she quickly blinked tears away. "I love when you call me Mom. Seriously. This is the best. I'm so proud of you. And yet I feel like I'm going to throw up because this is crazy. You can't leave us."

"Mom."

Sierra Montgomery wasn't my biological mother. But she had raised me since I'd first shown up in her life. She had been the first person I saw when I moved to Denver, lost, seemingly orphaned, and sitting on the stoop of my father's tattoo shop waiting for him to find me.

I had run from the authorities and other people watching me because I hadn't wanted to stay with them. I'd wanted to go with the man my mother had called my father until I'd learned the truth. And in the end, she had willed me to him anyway, so I hadn't even had to run from the authorities. I had just had to wait for them to contact him.

I had been too young to understand the legalities of everything, and yet I had run home to him. To a man who hadn't known me for the first ten years of my life, because he hadn't known I existed.

And now, as I looked up at the woman who had been by his side, I couldn't help but hold out my arms.

My mother, maybe not the one who had given birth to me, but the woman who had raised me, wrapped her arms around my waist and let out a shaky breath.

"I love you so much, Leif. You're my baby boy." She pulled back and wiped her tears. "Okay, *one* of my babies."

"At least the youngest two aren't bottle-fed anymore. So you'll be fine with that. And I expect daily photos and progress of when they're getting ready for their first day of preschool."

I couldn't believe I would miss that, but I needed to go. It was time for me to move out. I was twenty-one now. Old enough to drink in the United States, yet I was leaving the country to study abroad in Paris. I had gotten an internship with an art program there, and I was going to study art.

Art school here was working out well, and I love being creative, but learning from a master in Paris and being outside of Denver for the first time in my life for longer than a weekend or a week's vacation was going to be a new experience. At least, that's what I kept having to tell myself.

My three siblings ran into the room, laughing. Okay, Colin ran in while Gideon and Jamie toddled. I went down to my knees and held them all close.

Colin was nearly eight now and hugged me tight as the toddlers giggled into me.

I knew Gideon and Jamie understood I was leaving, but I didn't know if they knew what leaving meant.

But I hoped that video calls and constant messaging would make it feel like I wasn't that far from them. And that I wouldn't be missing so much of their lives.

I didn't like that I was leaving my family, but it would be nice to be somewhere where I wasn't a Montgomery. Because we were vast, and I wanted to see who I was when no one knew the name.

My father walked in then, broad, big, muscled, inked, bearded, and with an eyebrow ring glinting under the light.

He had been a baby when he'd had me and was still damn young, without a single gray hair in his beard or hair.

I wasn't sure how he did it, and I knew he didn't dye it at all. But he did not look his age. Neither did my mother. Hell, neither did my aunts or uncles or cousins. Everyone looked damn good, and I hoped that those Montgomery genes worked when it came to me.

I looked around then as I stood up, one kid on each leg as Colin wrapped his arm around my waist.

"I'm not going to be gone long. You're going to hear from me every day."

"You don't have to video chat every day, but at least a text," Dad said, and Mom scowled.

"Don't tell him not to call us, Austin. I want to hear from our boy daily."

"And we're not going to smother him, Sierra," he said softly as he held her close.

The love that they had nearly broke me.

These were the two that had raised me. The two that had shown me what it meant to care for another human and to hold that person in your soul.

I didn't think I'd ever find that for myself, not really. What they had was special.

I wasn't sure I was ready for something like that.

Especially not with what might be waiting for me when I returned home.

If I came home.

But I turned those thoughts away and held out my arms

to my family as they asked me about exactly what I was planning and the first thing I wanted to do when I got to Paris.

Today was going to be hard. Saying goodbye, knowing that anything could happen in a year.

I had to hope that would be enough time.

Enough time to fix everything.

Enough time to not be worried anymore.

Until then, I would figure out exactly what I wanted.

And I wouldn't be a Montgomery.

At least until I came home.

****

This isn't the end of the Montgomerys.

Leif Montgomery is next in Bittersweet Promises!

WANT TO READ A SPECIAL BONUS EPILOGUE FEATURING ARCHER & KILLIAN CLICK HERE!

A Note from Carrie Ann Ryan

Thank you so much for reading **INKED TEMPTATION!**

This book was a long time coming. I knew I'd wanted to write Archer's story long before I'd even met him. Having his story be the final book in this generation was exactly what I needed as an author.

I love writing this family. I feel like I'm part of theirs, or perhaps they're a part of mine. I've been blessed to write their stories and as you can tell, I don't plan on leaving them any time soon.

Somehow a few of the Montgomery kids are no longer kids! They're adults with lives, drama, and in need of HEAs. Leif is first, since of course he would be. His father started the series after all.

Leif's story brings us a new generation of Montgomerys, full of life, love, and cheese. Lake Montgomery is after him, the daughter of Arden and Liam from Wrapped in Ink. It's time to find out what happens when you're ready to find your happiness outside of the shadow of your amazing parents.

The Next Generation of Montgomerys deserve their stories beginning with BITTERSWEET PROMISES!

And since we're here...yes, the Wilder Brothers get a series, beginning with Eli's book, ONE WAY BACK TO ME.

The Montgomery Ink: Fort Collins Series:
Book 1: Inked Persuasion
Book 2: Inked Obsession
Book 3: Inked Devotion
Book 3.5: Nothing But Ink
Book 4: Inked Craving
Book 5: Inked Temptation

WANT TO READ A SPECIAL BONUS EPILOGUE FEATURING KILLIAN & ARCHER CLICK HERE!

If you want to make sure you know what's coming next from me, you can sign up for my newsletter at www.CarrieAnnRyan.com; follow me on twitter at @CarrieAnnRyan, or like my Facebook page. I also have a Facebook Fan Club where we have trivia, chats, and other goodies. You guys are the reason I get to do what I do and I thank you.

Make sure you're signed up for my MAILING LIST so you can know when the next releases are available as well as find giveaways and FREE READS.

Happy Reading!

Also from Carrie Ann Ryan

The Montgomery Ink Legacy Series:

Book 1: Bittersweet Promises

Book 2: At First Meet

Book 3: Longtime Crush

The Wilder Brothers Series:

Book 1: One Way Back to Me

Book 2: Always the One for Me

Book 3: The Path to You

Book 4: Coming Home for Us

The Aspen Pack Series:

Book 1: Etched in Honor

Book 2: Hunted in Darkness

Book 3: Mated in Chaos

Book 4: Harbored in Silence

The Montgomery Ink: Fort Collins Series:

Book 1: Inked Persuasion

Book 2: Inked Obsession

Book 3: Inked Devotion

Book 3.5: Nothing But Ink

Book 4: Inked Craving

Book 5: Inked Temptation

The Montgomery Ink: Boulder Series:

Book 1: Wrapped in Ink

Book 2: Sated in Ink

Book 3: Embraced in Ink

Book 3: Moments in Ink

Book 4: Seduced in Ink

Book 4.5: Captured in Ink

Book 4.7: Inked Fantasy

Book 4.8: A Very Montgomery Christmas

Montgomery Ink: Colorado Springs

Book 1: Fallen Ink

Book 2: Restless Ink

Book 2.5: Ashes to Ink

Book 3: Jagged Ink

Book 3.5: Ink by Numbers

Montgomery Ink Denver:

Book 0.5: Ink Inspired

Book 0.6: Ink Reunited

Book 1: Delicate Ink
Book 1.5: Forever Ink
Book 2: Tempting Boundaries
Book 3: Harder than Words
Book 3.5: Finally Found You
Book 4: Written in Ink
Book 4.5: Hidden Ink
Book 5: Ink Enduring
Book 6: Ink Exposed
Book 6.5: Adoring Ink
Book 6.6: Love, Honor, & Ink
Book 7: Inked Expressions
Book 7.3: Dropout
Book 7.5: Executive Ink
Book 8: Inked Memories
Book 8.5: Inked Nights
Book 8.7: Second Chance Ink
Book 8.5: Montgomery Midnight Kisses
Bonus: Inked Kingdom

The On My Own Series:

Book 0.5: My First Glance
Book 1: My One Night
Book 2: My Rebound
Book 3: My Next Play
Book 4: My Bad Decisions

The Promise Me Series:

Book 1: Forever Only Once
Book 2: From That Moment
Book 3: Far From Destined
Book 4: From Our First

The Less Than Series:
Book 1: Breathless With Her
Book 2: Reckless With You
Book 3: Shameless With Him

The Fractured Connections Series:
Book 1: Breaking Without You
Book 2: Shouldn't Have You
Book 3: Falling With You
Book 4: Taken With You

The Whiskey and Lies Series:
Book 1: Whiskey Secrets
Book 2: Whiskey Reveals
Book 3: Whiskey Undone

The Gallagher Brothers Series:
Book 1: Love Restored
Book 2: Passion Restored
Book 3: Hope Restored

The Ravenwood Coven Series:
Book 1: Dawn Unearthed

Book 2: Dusk Unveiled

Book 3: Evernight Unleashed

The Talon Pack:

Book 1: Tattered Loyalties

Book 2: An Alpha's Choice

Book 3: Mated in Mist

Book 4: Wolf Betrayed

Book 5: Fractured Silence

Book 6: Destiny Disgraced

Book 7: Eternal Mourning

Book 8: Strength Enduring

Book 9: Forever Broken

Book 10: Mated in Darkness

Book 11: Fated in Winter

Redwood Pack Series:

Book 1: An Alpha's Path

Book 2: A Taste for a Mate

Book 3: Trinity Bound

Book 3.5: A Night Away

Book 4: Enforcer's Redemption

Book 4.5: Blurred Expectations

Book 4.7: Forgiveness

Book 5: Shattered Emotions

Book 6: Hidden Destiny

Book 6.5: A Beta's Haven

Book 7: Fighting Fate

Book 7.5: Loving the Omega
Book 7.7: The Hunted Heart
Book 8: Wicked Wolf

The Elements of Five Series:
Book 1: From Breath and Ruin
Book 2: From Flame and Ash
Book 3: From Spirit and Binding
Book 4: From Shadow and Silence

Dante's Circle Series:
Book 1: Dust of My Wings
Book 2: Her Warriors' Three Wishes
Book 3: An Unlucky Moon
Book 3.5: His Choice
Book 4: Tangled Innocence
Book 5: Fierce Enchantment
Book 6: An Immortal's Song
Book 7: Prowled Darkness
Book 8: Dante's Circle Reborn

Holiday, Montana Series:
Book 1: Charmed Spirits
Book 2: Santa's Executive
Book 3: Finding Abigail
Book 4: Her Lucky Love
Book 5: Dreams of Ivory

The Branded Pack Series:
(Written with Alexandra Ivy)
Book 1: Stolen and Forgiven
Book 2: Abandoned and Unseen
Book 3: Buried and Shadowed

About the Author

Carrie Ann Ryan is the New York Times and USA Today bestselling author of contemporary, paranormal, and young adult romance. Her works include the Montgomery Ink, Redwood Pack, Fractured Connections, and Elements of Five series, which have sold over 3.0 million books worldwide. She started writing while in graduate school for her advanced degree in chemistry and hasn't stopped since. Carrie Ann has written over seventy-five novels and novellas with more in the works. When she's not losing herself in her emotional and action-packed worlds, she's reading as much as she can while wrangling her clowder of cats who have more followers than she does.

www.CarrieAnnRyan.com

Made in the USA
Coppell, TX
02 July 2022

79486393R00164